Moments in the

Private Room

Kudzai. R. Mhangwa

First published in Great Britain in 2023 by:

Carnelian Heart Publishing Ltd
Suite A
82 James Carter Road
Mildenhall
Suffolk
IP28 7DE
UK

www.carnelianheartpublishing.co.uk

Paperback ISBN   978-1-914287-42-8
eBook ISBN   978-1-914287-43-5

A CIP catalogue record for this book is available from the British Library.

Editors:
Lazarus Panashe Nyagwambo &
Samantha Rumbidzai Vazhure

Cover design & Layout:
Rukodzi Art &
Rebeca Covers

Typeset by Carnelian Heart Publishing Ltd
Layout and formatting by DanTs Media

To young women all over: may the complex women in this collection highlight your own beautiful complexity as a human being.

The truth is more peculiar than fiction. Life is really a startling place

      – Mira Nair

Table of Contents

FAMILY AFFAIRS

The evening was beautiful at the Meikles Hotel. One of their private reception rooms was elegantly decorated for the Marufus' cocktail party. It was past seven when Mufaro arrived. She made her way down the sea of carpet in the reception to ask the middle-aged receptionist where the party was being held. He went through the slow desktop in front of him until his eyes lit up when he found the information Mufaro had requested. She was directed to a room that was on the first floor.

Mufaro started up the stairwell. She considered it lazy to use an overworked elevator to reach the next floor even while wearing her sharply pointed stilettos. The shoes matched the red of her blouse, which was tucked into an African print pencil skirt. She had not had the chance to go home so she freshened up in the bathroom at work. She rinsed her mouth, ran water through her afro and combed out the small particles that had clung to it. She used a wet wipe to remove her makeup before dabbing Vaseline on her lips. She had arrived a little after the scheduled start time.

After reaching the first floor, she walked quickly, propelled by her paralysing fear of being late. As she walked through the door, she found the hall filled with people. She was welcomed by jazzy melodies from across the room. Through the smartly dressed people that were walking around like motiveless ants, she saw a band absorbed by their music. She walked around slowly, surveying the scene, noting the table filled with a kaleidoscope of food, the large glasses of champagne bubbling away and the colourful dresses and suits that the guests wore. It seemed so wasteful to her when just outside the building there were people that could not afford a single meal for themselves and their families. She circled the room looking for her parents. She felt herself getting hungry and decided to get food.

She was spoiled for choice; Swedish meatballs that smelt of thyme, cheese puff tarts, asparagus, tantalising rosemary ranch chicken skewers, spring rolls, samosas and devilled eggs. Mufaro picked up two eggs, placing them on a crisp napkin. She finally caught sight of her mother and father across the room, close to the stage where the tribute band was playing. She walked over to them and greeted them warmly.

"Hello, Mufaro, when did you get here?" her mother asked warmly.

"I arrived a few minutes ago. I got caught up at the office."

Her father was holding a half empty glass of beer.

"Ah! The office can wait! We need you here," her father said drunkenly. He notoriously could not control his drinking, even at the parties he hosted at their home. Whenever he got drunk, Mrs Marufu would lead him away from the party and retire him upstairs.

Mufaro ate one of the devilled eggs on the napkin, chewing it slowly trying to taste each spice that was in the filling. To her dismay, she could taste nothing.

"Are you going to eat that without a drink?" Mrs Marufu asked.

"No, I will get one later."

"You will choke on those eggs. You should have a drink. All of this was paid for, all of it!" Mr Marufu announced boastfully. He was often mocked for being "new money" but it was a disgrace that he learned to live with.

Mrs Marufu suggested that they interact with the other guests, but Mufaro was not in the mood to play host. She knew she would have to get back into the office early if she wanted to finish her work and a night spent entertaining her parent's plastic friends would drain her. She decided to get a lemon and lime mocktail.

The room was filled with people who had frequented her house for years; business partners and a few relatives. Mufaro and her sister Ndapiwa were expected to put on nice dresses and play the part of well-groomed daughters. She did not know where to start, so she went to one corner of the room where she stood sipping her mocktail slowly.

A face approached her from the crowd. It took her some time for it to register in her mind. It was Fadzai, an old acquaintance of hers from her teenage years.

"Mufaro Marufu, what a surprise to see you here." He was tall and scrawny and in his black suit and a black turtleneck jersey, he looked even skinnier.

"I'm surprised to see you too. How are you?" She wanted to say his name but decided not to.

"I'm doing okay. You look very different."

"Different how?" she said with demureness in her tone.

"I don't know. You look older I suppose."

"You look older too Fadzai. So tell me, how was your time in America?" Fadzai had gone to the United States to study criminal law.

"It went well I suppose." He sipped from the glass of champagne. "But I couldn't stand it there. You can barely find any intellectuals that could challenge my thinking over there so I decided to come back and you know, 'help rebuild our country.'" Fadzai's American accent was forced, which irritated Mufaro. "What about you? What happened to you after high school?"

She was caught off guard by his question.

"Well, I went to the Warwick School of Business then I came back here. I finished about two years ago."

"Came to help our country too?"

No, returned to work for my country, she thought. "You can say that. My father had already secured a position for me at his construction company, but business was struggling so I decided to find another territory to explore." She left out the part about her unwillingness to have everything handed to her on a silver platter by her father.

"So what are you doing now?"

"I'm trying to open a consultancy firm to help female entrepreneurs."

"That's very noble of you." He took another sip of his champagne and looked away. He bit his lower lip. Mufaro could see his yellow-stained teeth from cigarettes. His hair looked like it was slowly dying on his head.

"But it's so hard to get funding, particularly for women. That's one thing I will try and solve when the company is up and running."

"Funding? Can't your father help you?"

"I refused to let him. I want to do it alone. Can't be spoon-fed till I die, can I?"

"Wow. I would appreciate having a rich daddy. You should appreciate what you have. I bet your life is like Christmas every day." He started to back away from her.

"You know what, I think I should get some more food before it's finished. It was nice catching up with you," said Fadzai who was now a few steps away from her.

"That is a good idea. It was nice talking to you. We should speak again before you leave."

"Sure."

The tribute band had finished playing a song. A few people clapped their hands. They quickly went into their next song, 'Another sad love song' by Toni Braxton. The saxophone player took the lead playing the melody. Mufaro smiled in approval and moved towards the stage.

She heard her mother calling her from across the room. She approached her mother and father who were speaking to a chubby, charcoal-skinned man with a thick beard. He had a layered neck that looked like it was heavy on his chest.

"You remember the Minister, don't you?" Mrs Marufu asked. Mufaro tried to remember the man before she opened her mouth to speak.

"Of course I do," she lied, "How are you sir?" She stretched her hand to greet him. His palm was sweaty in hers.

"You've changed from when I last saw you," the Minister said.

"My girls have grown since you last saw them. Sometimes I can't recognise them myself," Mr Marufu said, his breath a mist of alcohol.

"The Minister was eager to see you when he arrived," Mrs Marufu said. Mufaro was handed a glass of red wine by her mother.

"No thank you mama." She pushed the glass away. She'd never acquired the taste for wine.

"My dear, we're here to party! Have a glass of wine or two, it won't kill you!" Mr Marufu said. Mufaro accepted the glass and took a sip.

"How has the office been?" Mrs Marufu asked the Minister.

"It has been going well but quite slowly, you know what it's like in an economy like this. It's hard to get any meaningful work done. We need more people like your daughter here to rebuild our country."

"People my age aren't interested in coming back to Zimbabwe. They want things to improve before they can decide if it's worth returning."

"It's you young people who should be leading the change. You can't wait for us *madhara* to bring change, can you?" he chuckled.

"That is true. But the problems are too enormous. They can't be solved in a day," Mrs Marufu said. She pretended to wave at a guest in the corner, took hold of her husband's shoulder and nudged him. "I think I see an old friend over there. We should go and see her. Minister, we will catch up later."

"That's okay Mrs Marufu, I'll be here with this beautiful gift you brought to this world."

"You are too kind," Mrs Marufu laughed.

The Minister moved closer to Mufaro. She brought her glass to her lips. Instead of drinking, she let the liquid move against her lips. The band finished playing 'Another sad love song'. Once again, only a few people applauded their performance. The next song was led by the pianist. Mufaro was impressed by how easily his fingers moved over the keys.

"The band plays very well, wouldn't you agree?" said Mufaro.

"Yes, I remember they played for us at a business lunch we had a few weeks ago. I was finishing a deal to bring in miners from China."

"China? They are willing to invest in the country at this time when we don't even have our own currency and our economy is marred by a cash shortage?"

"More than willing. I was there myself when the deal was sealed. I can see a great future ahead."

"That's wonderful," she placed the glass against her lips again.

The Minister looked at her for a few seconds. Mufaro could see him from her peripheral vision.

"Is there something wrong with my face?"

"No. I am just admiring you before I have to leave you."

Mufaro bit her lip. She felt some of the droplets of wine settle on her tongue. "How are your wife and children doing?"

"We are not here to talk about them, that's a conversation for another day. I am more interested in you. I'm told that you are starting your own business."

"Yes I am. It's still in the initial stages, but I'm sure that it will be on its feet in no time."

"With brains like yours it will stand the test of time."

"Thank you Minister. If you'll excuse me, I'd like to get some food."

"Allow me to get it for you…" he started to walk. She lightly placed her left hand on his arm. His suit felt soft. It was made of silk.

"Don't bother yourself. I'll manage," she walked quickly across the room to the table that had been replenished with food. She placed her glass of wine on the edge and picked up a napkin. She picked up some more devilled eggs and the samosas. She ate each one slowly, still trying to get some flavour from the eggs with no success. Mrs Marufu approached her.

"You and the Minister seemed to have a lovely conversation." She chirped as she picked up a meatball.

"Yes, he told me of a new deal that he signed with the Chinese. It's shocking how many deals he can get just because of his position."

"Well…" She dragged out the syllable. "You can get anything you want in this town if you are willing to pay the right price."

Mufaro looked around the room, studying the different faces around her.

"Your father has been trying to get a contract recently. Were you aware?"

"No, I haven't been very interested in *baba's* endeavours of late."

"It's such a shame, you know? We really looked forward to your participation in the business. Your intelligence is priceless."

"My brain or my body?" Something shifted between them. The air lost its dampness and the music seemed to get slower.

"Just help your father out this once. Please!" Mrs Marufu's throat was dry.

"He calls himself such a powerful businessman, why can't he seal a deal with his own efforts rather than getting drunk and making a fool of himself each time we have one of these parties?"

"You know this is essential. We need this deal and you could be very helpful."

Helpful? She wanted to move away from her mother immediately. She did not want to be reminded how her father had grown up with a single pair of shoes, or how not everything he had achieved was done ethically.

"Have you ever taken a close look at the Minister?" Mufaro asked stingingly.

"What are you talking about?"

"Exactly!"

Mufaro made her way to the cocktail bar once again to get herself a drink. She got a juicy pear mocktail. She decided to make her way home after finishing the drink. As she walked towards the entrance, she saw a coffee-complexioned vision that always looked new every time they saw each other. It was her sister, Ndapiwa.

Ndapiwa walked slowly, greeting each person she passed. She was wearing a royal blue evening gown with mermaid sleeves that were eager to slip off her pebble smooth shoulders. Around her neck was a cascading diamond necklace that sparkled when it caught the light. She always wanted to make sure that her presence was felt by everyone. Ndapiwa moved towards her parents who were speaking to the Minister once again. She greeted her parents with a kiss and the Minister with a handshake. Mufaro quickly made her way across the room towards them before their conversation started.

"I thought you weren't coming," Mufaro said to her sister.

"Why wouldn't I come?" Ndapiwa's voice was icy.

"Mr Marufu, you are so blessed to be surrounded by such beauty. From your wife to your daughters." It was the Minister.

The quartet laughed and Mr Marufu let out a spray of saliva. Some of it landed on Mufaro's cheek. She swept it off before looking at her sister from head to toe twice. Ndapiwa had a well-shaped oval face and tonight she had let her sheen Senegalese braids fall over her back. Mufaro felt envy creeping into her heart.

"You are far too kind, Minister. Are you enjoying yourself?" Ndapiwa asked.

"Of course. And with you now here, the party can only get better."

This time, it was only Ndapiwa and Mrs Marufu who giggled. Mr Marufu was now completely drunk and could not keep up with the conversation.

"If you'll excuse us," Mrs Marufu said, "we have to speak to some work mates over there." She dragged her husband away by his shoulder.

"Minister, I read about the Chinese coming to invest in the country. You never cease to amaze me." Ndapiwa said, pulling back her braids.

"It's all in a day's work. But the way you are running your father's empire," he wagged a finger at her, "I still can't put a finger on how you do it."

Ndapiwa let out a laugh, "Well… it's all in a day's work."

She and the Minister laughed while Mufaro finished her drink.

"But seriously, we could use someone like you in politics."

"Oh no! I've already found my place here. That's not an arena I would like to venture into."

"Think about it my girl."

"Would you like me to get you a drink when I get mine Mufaro?" Ndapiwa said.

"No, don't worry about me, I'm fine."

Mufaro walked away quickly. She watched from across the room as her sister spoke to the Minister. Ndapiwa's smile was electrifying and exhibited true glee. Mufaro wanted to reach out to her sister and pull her away. She looked as if she could float across the room with her mermaid dress. Mufaro decided to listen to the jazz band. She could not make out the song they were playing.

Ndapiwa walked over to where her sister was and handed her a glass filled with a dark red liquid. Mufaro gave her a questioning eye.

"Are you joking?"

"Relax, it's just grape juice."

Mufaro accepted the glass and took a short sip. She found herself looking at her sister once again who was sipping champagne.

"What brand is that?"

"What?"

"The champagne. What brand is it?"

"*Moet*. You know I don't drink any other brand. Would you like a taste?" Ndapiwa downed the bubbling liquid.

"Of course not. I was just curious."

"Curiosity is very suspicious in my book. Why be so curious and end up not trying?"

Mufaro was already growing tired of speaking to her sister. She looked around the room aimlessly.

"Are you alright?" asked Ndapiwa.

"I'm fine"

"You haven't done it have you?"

"Done what?"

"Really Mufaro? Have you helped our dear father secure his precious contract?"

Mufaro looked sharply at her sister. Their eyes spoke to each other for a moment.

"It's clear you haven't. If you had, that poor man would not be chatting me up like that, he's desperate to pull down his zipper I can tell you that."

"Ndapiwa." It was a whisper, "Anywhere but here. You cannot say that around people!"

"Would you like a little privacy?"

"I would like for this conversation to end."

"I'm sorry but you have to face reality. You know it's the only way we can get anything done in this world?"

"What do you mean by we?"

"We as women. Look at you, how many people are willing to help you with your new company? If it was a man doing the same, he wouldn't struggle this much."

"If that's true, why hasn't your beloved father got the contract yet?" Mufaro felt her temples throb.

"Because it isn't that simple. You act as if you don't know how it works around here."

"I know how it works Ndapiwa, but it shouldn't have to be that way."

"Oh stop it Mufaro. Petty excuses for your lack of bravery"

"Then I'd rather be a coward. Always remember that you have always been the cheap one between us."

Ndapiwa looked directly at her sister, studying each feature of her face carefully. She was about to speak when Fadzai came out of nowhere and greeted her. Mufaro forced down her drink, trying to ignore Fadzai's forced accent and her sister's girlish laughter. Mufaro decided to leave the party. At the large entrance, she met the Minister.

"Leaving so soon?"

"Yes, I have a busy day tomorrow."

"I was hoping we could have some time to ourselves before you left."

"Minister, I don't think this is appropriate."

"What a man feels for a woman is inappropriate? Come on, you are such a beautiful girl and I couldn't keep my eyes off you the whole night. It's like you were growing more beautiful the more I saw you"

"Minister…"

"I've booked a room upstairs. We can share wine and look at the stars until the sun rises my girl. And it won't be the only time we will meet. I want to make you mine Mufaro. Now let's go, shall we?"

Mufaro was uncertain what to say. She felt as if she was about to burst into tears. She left the Minister and found herself in the bathroom. She allowed herself to cry, but she was not crying for herself. What she was crying for was bigger than her. She cried for power.

She dried her tears in front of the mirror, taking her time using the rough paper towels that were meant for wiping hands. Mufaro left the bathroom and walked down the stairs to the lobby. Across the room, she saw Ndapiwa and the Minister walking up the stairs.

She wanted to catch her sister's eye one more time. She felt like grabbing her heart and unleashing her warmth on her. They disappeared into the shadow of the hallway. Mufaro stood in the middle of the dusty lobby, her mind lost somewhere she did not know. She decided to return to the party. She went to the cocktail table and asked for red wine. She took small sips, allowing the liquid to discover her throat slowly. Mrs Marufu came towards her.

"Hello my dear. It's almost 11 pm."

"Don't worry it's done," Mufaro said before taking another sip.

Mrs Marufu patted her daughter's right shoulder and left.

Ndapiwa came back to the party an hour later. Mufaro approached her with a glass filled with wine.

"Would you like a drink before we leave?"

STOP THE PRESSES

Bongi decided to launch her magazine after she had tried to buy one at the supermarket. As her eyes searched across the wooden stall, she was disappointed because she did not see anybody that looked like her on the shiny covers. All of the women were born of winter, their skin made even lighter by camera effects. She picked up a décor magazine instead, that she never bothered to read when she arrived back at her flat.

She mapped out the magazine on scraps of paper in her home office, visualising how it would look, the images she would include, the articles she would feature and how it would feel when you held it. She set up a Facebook page that night with a post calling on writers to send in their pieces for consideration.

The following weeks were spent picking up as many old magazines as she could get her hands on. She chose the magazines very carefully; *Essence* was the most sought after publication followed by *Ebony*. She also favoured *Drum* magazine, *Cosmopolitan*, *Glamour*, *Vanity Fair* and *Jet*. There were a few issues of the Oprah magazine. They were all piled up in a corner of her bedroom. Bongi then tore through them each night determinedly. She cut out certain articles and placed them in a folder to serve as a guideline. She would name the magazine *Buhle*, meaning beauty in the Ndebele language.

The first person to contact her on Facebook was Sheila, a former schoolmate of Bongi's. She said she was enthusiastic about the idea and wanted to help her with the magazine. She had a degree in communications and media from the University of Namibia. Bongi agreed to meet with Sheila for coffee.

Sheila was autumn when it reluctantly turned into winter, her skin matching the cappuccino she cradled with both hands as Bongi explained her vision for the magazine.

"So, what's going to be the mission statement for the magazine?"

"Love notes to a sister. It is what I wish I had heard when I was younger."

Sheila was impressed, as Bongi talked more about what she wanted to do, offering the occasional "ahs" and nodding her head when it was necessary.

"I love the idea and I think it will work well, but I suggest we do not make it too indigenous," Sheila suggested.

"I don't understand."

"You know how we are in this country, we are so attracted to foreign things. We have to make sure that we have an international appeal to get more people to read it."

"I'll take note of that."

They left the café around mid-afternoon. Sheila was the first to walk out into the blanket of sunshine. She put on her beige sun hat.

"Your skin is flawless Sheila."

"Thank you," she said coyly, "It's these new creams I'm using. I have to stay out of the sun though. I can give you the contact of the woman I buy the creams from. Her name is Prudence. She makes them herself and she is still working on getting exposure, the magazine could help her." Bongi agreed.

The initially slow responses to the call for articles began to pick up after a month. Bongi read through them at night when she came home from work. Most of the articles underwhelmed her; they lacked the incandescent spirit she wanted to run through the entire magazine.

In the first issue she was going to include an interview with a local filmmaker. A segment featuring a fashion designer who had just displayed her line in Nigeria was going to be featured and a cosmetologist had submitted relationship tips although they would have to be revised because some of the content was too provocative. Bongi decided to do the book review segment herself. When Sheila had gone through the article, she decided to add a few international books.

"I had wanted to feature only local authors. Give them a chance at some exposure."

"Yes, but we must also include international authors. *That* will get people reading that segment."

Bongi relented and allowed Sheila to include three international bestselling titles, removing three novels by Zimbabwean authors. Bongi had to apologise to the authors and promised to feature their books in future publications.

One night Bongi received a poster from Prudence, the woman who made the skin cream Sheila had endorsed. It featured a fair skinned model smiling broadly against a dusty pink backdrop. The words "A gentle kiss from nature" ran across the top in a jarringly cursive font. Bongi dialled Sheila's phone number.

"It's almost 10 pm, don't you rest?" Sheila was trying not to sound angry.

"I'm having doubts about including a poster for lightening creams in the magazine."

"Why?"

"Do you think this is something we should include in the magazine?"

"Why not? Adverts are necessary."

"Does it have to be this one?"

"She said she'd pay us, so yes." Sheila yawned, "So will you let me sleep now?"

One day, Bongi received a care package from Prudence. It was filled with scented candles, bath soaps and lightening cream. She dabbed some of the cream onto the back of her hand. It had a strong citrusy smell and felt slimy on her skin. Bongi washed it off immediately. "Thank you for your vision," the accompanying note read. Looking at the clock, she decided it would be an acceptable time to call Sheila.

"I received a call from the woman who is supposed to write our motivational piece. She said she won't be able to submit her article on time." Bongi's voice was higher than usual as she spoke to Sheila.

"What was her stupid excuse?" said Sheila.

"She didn't give me one. Now I'm stuck."

"Why don't you write the motivational piece yourself?"

"Me?"

"Of course! You launched a magazine from the ground up and you're working to the bone to make it a success. That's worth writing about."

Bongi liked the idea. She started work on it that night.

Our very first motivation corner comes from me, the founder and editor of Buhle.

This is a magazine for women, by women and with women in mind and at heart. Think of it as a special note from an older sister! We want to change the way that we, as African women, see ourselves and the way the world sees us with this publication. It's time we brought our own chairs to the table and not wait for someone else to offer them to us. So here it is! This magazine was born from a place of rage…

A few weeks before the magazine was due for publication, Sheila was showing Bongi a sample that a graphic designer had prepared for them

"He is a genius! He was really able to capture my essence," said Bongi. "There is one more thing I want to include; I have a friend who works for an environmental management firm and they are having this petition signed to stop a construction company from building an office complex on a wetland in the eastern suburbs."

"You wanted to include that in the magazine?"

"They need a thousand signatures. Then they plan to have a protest march. He is hoping we will boost support for them."

"It might be risky to become too political in the first issue."

"It's nothing political, it's an environmental issue."

"But people will take as if we are taking sides. What is the name of the company?"

"I can't even pronounce it. It's a company from Singapore."

"Whatever the company's name, this doesn't concern the magazine."

The petition was excluded from the magazine.

I was tired of reading magazines that did not celebrate me as an authentic African citizen, more specifically as a Zimbabwean woman. I rarely saw people who looked like me when I read magazines or watched television. I felt invisible.

For the cover, they decided to put a jazz musician and spoken word artist named Cherish. Cherish's photo shoot was underway in the late morning, two weeks before the magazine was due for issuing. The photographer's studio was in a leafy suburb in Harare. It was an open plan building which overlooked the street below. The floors were littered with scraps of papers and photo negatives and the walls of the studio had black and white portraits of models. Sheila arrived about halfway into the photo shoot. She was wearing a black sun hat with a white bow, her eyes hidden behind large sunglasses.

"Can we do something about her hair?" asked Sheila.

"What?"

"Cherish's hair. Can we do something about it?"

"Would you like me to comb it out more or perhaps I can style it? Or even put on a head wrap? I always carry a few head wraps in my bag," Cherish was instantly apologetic.

"No, can we put a weave on you? Or even relax it."

"That would take ages to get done and we're already halfway through." This was the photographer, allowing the Canon camera to hang off the front of her neck. "We need to get these pictures done by end of week."

"Can't you work through the night?" It was more of a command than a sincere question. "We can't put her on the cover with that afro. The picture might not even fit on the cover with how fanned out it is." Sheila's argument did not make sense to Bongi.

Cherish eventually agreed to have the weave done. The photographer agreed to do the photoshoot into the night.

Bongi and Sheila stood in front of the salon as Cherish got her hair done by two hairdressers.

"There was nothing wrong with her hair. It's who she is as an artist," Bongi said to Sheila.

"People don't want to see that on the front cover of a magazine."

"See what? A woman with the hair that God gave her?"

That evening Sheila was at Bongi's flat. The magazines that Bongi had collected were spread out on the floor. Sheila was analysing each of the magazines for Bongi, her finger jumping from one publication to the next.

"You see what I mean? All of these women have their hair done or styled. Even on Oprah's magazine! People will buy an image, not authenticity. Give them what they think is beautiful, not what they want to be beautiful."

Bongi just wanted the conversation to stop. She almost felt dizzy looking at the different faces on the magazines.

I was one of the darkest people when I was in high school. This automatically meant I was the proverbial ugly duckling, the girl who never got asked out and was the subject of any joke related to skin colour. I had to find my way out of this. This is why I founded this magazine. There is a place in this world for me and countless other women who think of themselves as un-beautiful. There is nothing in this world – especially something as trivial as skin colour – that will stop you from reaching for the stars. Enjoy!

A copy of the printed magazine was sent to Bongi one Saturday afternoon for proofreading. There it was; the words *Buhle* in carnation-white sliding from left to right at the top of the magazine. Cherish looked up at her, a broad smile on her face. The weave looked curly and framed her oval face perfectly. She took a look at the headlines around the magazine.

"Cherish – ready to redefine Afro-Jazz forever!"

"Rekindling your passion"

"Latest fashion tips and tricks"

"Local filmmaker on his career and life"

"Top Ten tips for the career girl"

"Auntie Julie to the rescue!"

She perused through the pages, carefully going through each article and making sure the layout was perfect and the pictures were clear. Sheila rang just as she put the magazine down.

"I assume you've gone through the magazine," Sheila sounded excited.

"It's nice."

"Nice? It's perfect! It's hitting shelves in one week. Did you notice any errors?"

"No I didn't. Did you?"

"Your motivational piece, could you change it? I don't think it would be appropriate to talk about your childhood trauma, focus more on your struggle setting up the magazine. Oh, and say co-founder, not founder."

"The magazine *was* born from my childhood trauma. That's why I talked about my struggle with appearance. Maybe you don't understand how it is to be ridiculed for being who you are but I do, and I'm sure that countless others will relate to that."

"The point of the piece is to encourage more people to move forward to achieve their dreams. It's not fitting to talk about skin colour. That's a sensitive issue and you should know better. Just work on it, okay? I also have good news! Prudence has decided to be a sponsor. She said she would donate some care packages for the next issue. I think for the next cover we can put someone who isn't so roughed up, someone exotic! Those fair skinned Ethiopian beauties that are trending these days."

Bongi left the phone and went to the bathroom. She picked up one of the lightening creams. She found the décor magazine she bought at the supermarket the day she decided to start *Buhle* and went back to the kitchen table. The line had cut. The first page of the home magazine had the story of a woman whose house had burned down and how she had worked hard to rebuild it. She took some of the cream and rubbed it onto the back of her hand.

THESE STREETS

The man had been waiting for what felt like hours for Chengeto to leave her house. They had messaged each other by SMS and agreed they would meet at 7 pm after his shift from work was over. The time now read 8:23 pm. The lights inside Chengeto's house were on, so he knew she was inside. A few people had passed by the man's white Mazda 3, eyeing him suspiciously. He did not blame them for doing so. There had been an increase in abductions in recent months according to a police report he had heard over the radio.

When the clock struck 8:30 pm, he decided to send a text.

I don't appreciate you wasting my time the way you did today. You really disappointed me.

He looked back at the two bottles of Heineken that were on the back seat. Chengeto had told him she did not take beer well, but the man knew it would help loosen her up. He switched his car into life and went on his way. It was not a complete loss; his wife was at home waiting for him. Chengeto was his younger mistress. She did not know that he was a married man. They had been lovers for close to two months now and the man could tell she was falling in love with him from the flowery texts she was sending him of late.

He drove at high speed, thinking of how he was going to ignore Chengeto for the next few days. He would call her later and complain about how she did not value him. *It was too easy with these young girls.* As he made the turn into the Kuwadzana roundabout, he saw a woman standing under a tree. She was so thin, the outline of her skeleton was like a sculpture; she was wearing a wrap dress made of shiny fabric and her dreadlocks stretched below her backside with shells attached to the tips. The man gradually stopped his car.

"Ambuya? Hamusi kutonhorwa?"

"No, I'm not cold at all," her voice was high pitched.

"Can I give you a lift?"

She had already opened the passenger door before she accepted the offer. It was unlike him to help a stranger on the street in pitch black night. However, his need for companionship made him pick the woman up.

"Where shall I drop you off?"

"I'll show you when we get there," she replied curtly.

They cruised smoothly down the road for a while, not speaking. The man took a good look at her and he was sure she had noticed his gaze. They sat in silence for a short while until she began the conversation.

"Where are you coming from so late at night?" she started.

"I had some work to finish off and it took some time. I'm an accountant, so I'm usually the last person to leave the building," this was the exact same lie he told his wife whenever he visited Chengeto or any of the other girls he went out with. It always worked well.

"Hoo saka muri vemari ka?"

He giggled, "Not exactly. I live a humble life. What about you?"

"Haa I do work here and there. Full time employment is hard to come by these days."

"So, are you coming from work right now?"

"Something like that." She did not have a bag on her or any indication she was travelling.

The road was mostly clear at this time of night except for a few public transport operators. His phone began to buzz in his glove compartment. He pulled it out, its flashing bright green light momentarily lighting up his face as he flipped it open, and saw that it was Chengeto calling. The man was

eager to answer it and spit vile at the woman who had stood
him up, but he couldn't answer right then.

"People still have phones like that?" it was the woman
asking.

"Phones like what?"

She pointed at the Motorola V66 that the man had just
ignored. The device looked new.

"Yes, they're good on battery life."

"I'm sure there are smartphones good on battery life as
well."

The phone rang once again. He switched it off angrily and
put it back in the glove compartment.

"It's work," he said, addressing no one in particular.

"Sure about that?"

"Why do you ask?"

"It is written all over your face, you're angry with someone
you love."

He was surprised by her intuitiveness. But she was wrong;
he did not love Chengeto.

"No, it's work related."

"Okay. If you say so."

"Why do you think that?"

"You were so violent when you switched the phone off.
And why does it stay in the glove compartment? Is it because
you use it to contact *ma*girlfriend?"

"Between my wife and my work schedule I don't have
time for that."

He could tell, as the words left his mouth, that she did not
believe him. He did his best to keep his eyes on the road.

"It wouldn't be the strangest thing in the world, you
know? My own sister cheated on her husband with her
father-in-law."

"Women these days no longer have morals."

"Why were we expected to have morals all this time while you men could act like spoiled children? And that isn't even half of it. She got pregnant by the father-in-law and now her husband is raising the son as his own."

He looked at her in bewilderment.

"True story!"

"Wait until the husband finds out!"

"People get away with stories like this all the time, it will never come out. You men think you are clever, but we have you under our thumbs. Do you have children? You might be in the same situation as my brother-in-law." She smiled mischievously.

"I don't have children yet. I've been married for two years and my wife wants us to have some time to ourselves first."

She nodded and looked out of the window, watching the dim tower lights in the distance.

"When you do decide to have children, I hope you are lucky. I have an aunt who gave birth to a frog last year?"

This caught the man off guard. He almost swerved off the road into the bushes. He had never heard a story like that before. There was a local newspaper which told strange and bizarre stories such as these ones but he had never bought it because he thought it was a waste of his money.

"Frog!" the man exclaimed in disbelief.

"*Datya chairo*! I'm sorry I frightened you! I saw you almost had an accident."

"I almost had a heart attack, not an accident!"

"Both *saka*!" The woman laughed.

"Are you telling the truth?"

"I was there! We couldn't get her to the hospital on time, so she gave birth in her bedroom. I saw the frog come out between her legs with my own two eyes."

"*Munoreva nhema!*"

"I swear to God! We buried it but the chief found out. She got into trouble and ran away. To this day we don't know where she is."

"Maybe she ran away to South Africa. That's where everyone is going these days." He replied after a while.

"I never liked her that much, she can end up at Satan's feet for all I care. The sister-in-law I care for is the one in the UK. *Iro ndiro dhongi rangu!*"

The sister-in-law in question had gone to the UK on a tourist visa and never came back. She had left her five children in Zimbabwe and promised to bring them to the UK when she had enough money for their airfare. Her money was never enough though, because the woman kept demanding money for rent, clothes, shoes and jewellery from her in return for occasionally looking out for her children.

"She works hard but she and my brother were homeless when she first arrived in London. They seem to be on their feet now which is a good thing for me."

"Why don't you go there as well? Maybe you can run away from all of the scary tales that you are telling me tonight."

"You're frightened by what I told you? You haven't heard half of it!"

They were passing by a service station when the man instinctively checked his fuel gauge and saw that it was close to empty. He made a turn into the station. He told his passenger that he was going to fill up on petrol.

"Great! I need to use the restroom too."

He watched as the woman made her way into the service station's convenience store. He handed the fuel attendant a twenty-dollar bill and watched carefully as the liquid was poured into his car. For a moment he thought of leaving his passenger by the shop. He found her both strange and enthralling, more of the former. He suddenly found himself longing for Chengeto.

The fuel attendant had just finished fuelling up when the woman jumped back into the car with a newspaper under her armpit. They drove off. A new chill had settled on the night.

"I have a jacket in the back," the man said. "You could wear it if you'd like."

"No, don't worry about me," she said, her face glued to the newspaper on her lap. He was relieved he wouldn't need to talk to her for the remainder of their journey. Just as he eased into the rhythm of his drive she gasped. She turned the newspaper towards him and pointed at an article.

"Look!"

"The price of Pepsi has gone up?" he said dryly.

"No man! This headline, 'Livid Wife Arrested for slashing husband's face'... I know this woman. She lives close to us."

"Where is that?"

"*Ikoko uko*." she answered vaguely, "Her name is Tafadzwa. She is such a nice girl."

"Why would a nice girl slash someone else's face?"

"You don't know the whole story. Her husband did not want her leaving the house so she lived more or less like a prisoner. One afternoon she went along the whole street telling people that she was going to fix her husband. Little did we know she was going to do this! *Mashura aGeorgina*!"

"Were you there when she attacked her husband?"

"I and ten other neighbours. Serves him right for treating his wife like that!"

Suddenly, a thought occurred to him: if a woman could deface her husband for imprisoning her, what would she have done if she had found him cheating? What would happen if his own wife found him cheating?

They drove on, and the woman showed no signs that she would be disembarking soon. She did not even give the man directions. She kept talking about odd headlines as if she was a reporter.

"You should look for a job at ZBC as a news anchor," the man joked after she had told what felt like the millionth strange story he had heard that night.

"I would run all of the presenters out of their jobs," she quipped.

"*Ambuya imimi muri ve*controversy!" he declared.

"These are all stories that I have witnessed, I'm not involved in any of them sir!"

"Then what are you involved in?"

"You can leave me by that clearing over there." There was only a forest of maize crop that stretched on for miles. It looked unsafe.

"What are you going to do after I drop you off? No buses pass by here."

"Don't worry about me. It's you I'm worried about."

"Why?"

"*Mapfekero aya ndeechihure*! I know you had gone to see someone you are involved with." The man always cleaned up a little more when he went to see Chengeto. Tonight, he was wearing a faux leather jacket over a black turtleneck. He wore tight fitting jeans and the whole ensemble was completed by a pair of shiny glass dress shoes.

"It was casual Friday at work!"

"Sir, relax. Just relax."

"Could you be of any assistance?"

She rubbed his thigh. "It would be a pleasure."

He pulled down his pants slightly while she took him in. The man reclined his seat while the woman was at work, and he let her take control. When it was over, he wiped himself down and pulled up his pants hastily.

"Thank you so much for the ride. God bless and good night." She was already outside of the car. She looked at the car's number plates.

"I took your number plate so I can warn my friend who is a carjacker not to take yours!"

The man cruised up the road. He turned back to take one last look at his strange passenger. She was gone. Driving further into the darkness of the night, he wondered whether he should return Chengeto's calls or let her suffer for a while longer.

THE WOMAN WITH THE TWISTED HAIR

She always sat in the same pew at the cathedral, the second one from the entrance, and never uttered a word during the service. She only moved her lips, not letting any solid sentence take shape. *Does she actually know the order of mass, I wondered?*

She lived in the block of flats opposite the church building. The walls were muddied while the pipes were clogged and sang in ceaseless howl to the tune of rotten food and human waste. One day, I saw her getting her hair done by Rutendo whilst sitting under the mango tree. Rutendo also lived in the same block of flats. The woman's afro was combed out and fashioned into small twists. She handed Rutendo five US dollars when she was finished and walked away without saying a word.

Afterwards, I asked Rutendo what she knew about the woman. She told me she smelt of rose oil and that her hair was blanket-soft. She did not know the woman's name, even though she had done her hair a few times. She said the woman's speech was unordered, saying anything about anything at any time. One minute she would talk about the latest newspaper headline of a cheating wife being stabbed by her husband; the next moment she would complain about the rising prices of food; then she would say she was planning on getting a new antenna for her television.

There was a rumour that the woman had been deported from the United States, according to one branch of the grapevine, or the United Kingdom or France, according to others. Some said she was married to a rich white man. It was he who had given her the pure gold rings she wore on each finger of her left hand; the ring finger had an additional ring with a large jewel which shimmered like water teeming with algae. Even the clothes she wore looked expensive like they were Louis Vuitton or Versace or that brand I once saw in *Glamour* magazine but could not pronounce – Yves Saint Laurent.

Other people said she was a witch from Mutoko who had found herself in Harare. A family that lived in the same flats said they recognised her from one of their trips there for a funeral. They said she had gone mad from all the medicines she used on people and that she had used her witchcraft to get the flat she was living in. They also said she only went to church to cast spells on the people who attended mass. The blackness of her hands was the side effect of her medicines, according to these same people.

The man who sold newspapers on the street corner told me that he saw her dancing in her window one night, her arms outstretched as if she wanted to pull down the ceiling. He said she had looked like she was chewing on a hard piece of meat. Nobody ever took what he said seriously though. This was the man who once claimed that he attended the one o'clock mass - a service done in Portuguese that had been cancelled years ago.

Despite her eccentricity, her face was beautiful; round with large intelligent eyes and a well-sculpted nose that looked like the work of a plastic surgeon. I wanted to believe she came from the United States because I could imagine her in the glossy weaves that African-Americans wear.

One day when I went to get my own hair done by Rutendo, I met Mai Tendai who said she would clear up any rumours I had heard about the woman. Mai Tendai had something to say about the whole neighbourhood. Not a single week went by when she did not get into a scuffle or fight with another woman. She said the woman was a prostitute and that she barely spoke because she did not want people to find out. Mai Tendai swore on her late husband's grave that she was telling the truth. I accepted it.

Rutendo was late by ten minutes. As I stood waiting for her, I saw the woman with twisted hair walking towards me out of the corner of my eye. She asked to have her hair re-done. Her voice was like a muted trumpet. I calmly explained to her that I was not Rutendo, I was only a customer of hers. Her smooth forehead broke into gorges of frown lines and she spat out, "*Bien, alors j'irai!*" before storming off across the street. I knew she had spoken in French because I remembered my high school French teacher would write *bien* in my book when I scored at least 50%.

I finally came up with my own version of the woman's backstory; she had worked as a prostitute and exotic dancer in France before returning to Zimbabwe. She had practised witchcraft at some point in her life, but I was not sure when. That was the story I would tell others. I watched as she walked over to the mango tree, pick a mango and sit under its shade, sucking on the perfectly ripe fruit, her skin shining like a precious jewel.

I decided then that I would ask Rutendo to do my hair like that of the woman with the twisted hair.

A MURDER MYSTERY

It was a few minutes after seven in the evening when the detective left Dadirai's house. She had entertained him for about an hour, seated outside the complex she lived in, a cluster of twelve small flats. The flats were perfect rectangular-shaped boxes painted peach, each with two windows at the top. The garden at the back was small but well taken care of by the gardener who tended to it twice a week. There was a washing line which shone as if it was newly erected; Dadirai never made use of it, most of her clothes were sent to the cleaners. Once he had left, she went back to her house. As she stepped onto her unlit porch, she remembered the bulb she had forgotten to replace. She decided she would do it in the morning.

Judith was watching CNN on the large plasma screen. Dadirai poked the fire that was burning in the fireplace with a tong before joining Judith on the couch.

Judith switched off the television.

"Your television screen is too bright!" Judith complained.

"I've tried to adjust it, but I can't work the damn thing," Dadirai said. "The detective is finally gone, I was getting tired talking to him."

"I can imagine. It's not easy having to talk about your friend's death."

"I didn't want to but I had no other choice. I'm the only family she had in the city."

The stairs began to creak as Pamela descended them, her plump feet resting heavily on each step. She grabbed a tin of Pringles before sitting down with the two other women.

"Is the fine detective gone yet?" Pamela giggled, "Didn't you find him attractive?" She handed Dadirai the tin of Pringles which she poured out into her hand.

"I think Dadirai has other things to worry about besides how the detective looks," Judith said.

"Have they found anything yet concerning how Valerie was killed?" asked Pamela.

Dadirai told them there were no new developments at that point; they had only taken the body to the mortuary. Dadirai would go to Chivhu in the morning to tell Valerie's mother about the murder.

"It's a shame for such a young person to lose her life. They stab you and leave you on the floor of your own home. This world is full of sick people!" said Pamela, her mouth filled with the thin crisps.

"It was the boyfriend I'm sure." Judith and Pamela turned to Dadirai.

"How can you be so sure?" inquired Judith. Dadirai said that it was her sixth sense. Pamela sighed in disapproval.

"There goes psycho Dadi with her predictions!" said Judith.

"It's psychic! And didn't you know she had a new boyfriend from overseas?" Dadirai paused to catch her breath "He was a Canadian who had come to work for an NGO here. I met him at Sam Levi one day with Valerie when he'd taken her out for lunch. I can't remember his name. It was one of those odd names white people give their children."

Pamela and Judith looked at her, disbelief carved on their faces.

"A white boy?" cried Judith, "It can't be."

"Believe it or not, I saw them. A blue eyed, chalk white man!"

All three of them pushed themselves against the fake leather sofas and laughed loudly. Dadirai suddenly remembered the old woman from next door who always came to tell them they were making too much noise whenever she had her friends over. Pamela was almost choked by the chips in her mouth and coughed violently, banging her fist against her chest.

The women settled down.

"What makes you think he did it, Dadi?" asked Judith.

"He's nowhere to be found. The police think he might have left the country. If that isn't incriminating enough, I don't know what is."

Pamela cleared her throat, "She was a prisoner of her passions, desperately hoping for a romantic man who would take her to fine restaurants and candle lit dinners. I always used to tell her that it was one in a million! Now look what has happened to her."

Dadirai finally noticed that Judith had not been given the Pringles and handed her the almost empty tin. Judith picked through the crushed chips that were at the bottom.

"She probably thought this white boy of hers was going to take her to live in the Diaspora. Who would blame her? Zimbabwe isn't the best place to be of late."

"Pamela! You are still thinking of that? I thought we had moved on from that topic," Dadirai scolded her. Pamela turned to look at the painting that was hanging over the television.

Dadirai thought of her journey to the village to tell Valerie's mother about the death of her only daughter. She had been put out of her comfort zone, having to deal with the funeral arrangements.

"So we won't be seeing you at church tomorrow Dadi?" asked Judith.

"No, I'm going to be on the road to Chivhu by 6 am. I think it's best if I talk to Valerie's mother in person instead of over the phone."

"I can come with you if you want," offered Judith.

"Don't worry about that, I'll be fine."

"And you don't want to miss Pastor Cornelius preaching tomorrow, do you Judith?" asked Pamela.

"Is he back from his honeymoon in Hawaii ?" Dadirai interrupted.

"He came back last week with his new bride. Michelle is her name I think." Pamela said the name as if she was about to vomit. "They must have finished spending our offerings and tithes."

There was a silence before Dadirai broke into a giggle. She covered her thin lips with her hand, trying not to laugh out loud.

"Say what's on your mind, Dadi," Pamela urged. Dadirai screamed out Michelle's name and Pamela burst into laughter.

"That girl! She never used to talk to anyone until she got engaged to Cornelius. Now that she is married to the pastor's son, she tries to act like a proper lady. I remember when she asked our section to help her choose her gown. She arrived fifteen minutes late and had us all waiting to see her trying on those cheap gowns from China."

"You actually went for her gown fitting? Why didn't you tell me? I know it was pure drama. *Firimu chaiyo*! Tell us the details." Pamela's eyes came alive.

"Haa! She tried on three gowns but she didn't like any of them. She actually wanted us to attend another fitting the following week," Dadirai continued, "The other ladies were fed up with her so we made her choose that ugly frock she wore on the wedding day."

Judith watched the conversation quietly, the other women ignoring her as if she had evaporated into mist.

"Have you seen the way she dresses these days? She wears those tight clothes that don't even complement that disfigured body of hers," this was Pamela.

"What of her make up? Don't even get me started! *Chipoko*!" Pamela's eyes were welling up with tears.

"Ladies, ladies, ladies, maybe we should stop there," Judith interrupted.

Pamela and Dadirai quietened down.

"If you are looking for a killer, it's definitely Michelle?" Pamela said. The other two women cast her disapproving glances.

"*Nhai iwe*? Where do you get your ideas sometimes?" Dadirai scorned.

"Are you telling me you didn't know? Why, our church is a garden ripe with fresh gossip each week."

Judith focused on the painting, not wanting to take part in the conversation.

"Pamela just be straight with us," said Dadirai.

"Fine Dadi. The holy pastor and our dear Valerie were getting cosy in between his sheets."

After her announcement, Pamela gave a hearty laugh tilting her body backwards on the sofa.

"Pamela, this isn't funny."

"I'm not joking! Ever since Valerie was appointed secretary for the youth council haven't you noticed how she was always around the church? She and Cornelius have always had a strong attraction for each other, but he would never have married her. She lacked… what do you call it?" She snapped her fingers, "…Sophistication!"

From Judith and Dadirai's dazed expressions, Pamela thought they were picturing Cornelius, with his build like a wrestler, his unblemished dark-brown skin and sculpted face that made Valerie look twice.

"And who told you that rubbish?" asked Dadirai.

"Who carries around all the gossip of that church?"

Dadirai and Pamela laughed as if they were screaming while Judith smiled coyly.

There was suddenly a knock at the door. They knew it was Dadirai's neighbour who always complained about noise whenever the other two girls visited. The three women decided to keep quiet until she left the door. She knocked five more times before finally giving up. They laughed softly after the violent knocks had vanished.

"That woman is going to move out before I do. So who are you talking about? Mrs Huni?"

"Who else? She doesn't spend her time there helping around the church. She is always busy poking her nose where it shouldn't be. She is such a simple person despite her bank balance. She is the one who told me about Cornelius and Valerie sneaking around in the offices."

"It can't be!" Judith exclaimed. She was hushed by Dadirai.

"Valarie would do anything to get ahead in life. You might be right. Maybe Michelle sliced Valarie's throat to get her out of the picture. You never know."

The temperature began to drop as the minutes passed by. Dadirai went over to the fireplace to add the remaining pieces of wood to the dying fire.

"What if it wasn't Michelle?" Dadirai said.

"Who else could it be then?" Judith asked.

"It could be Cornelius."

"Cornelius is taking over from his father soon. He can't afford another blunder like what his father did a few years ago," said Dadirai.

"You mean the scandal of selling people those fake enchanted trinkets?" Judith recalled.

"No! Not that one," Dadirai admonished.

"Girls that church has had so many scandals it's hard to keep track."

"You see! And imagine the future leader of the church having to deal with a loose, unsophisticated mistress like our friend on the side?" Dadirai said pompously.

"He isn't capable of it! Never!" Pamela was nearly angry.

Judith sat trying to find something to add to the conversation. She was fond of Dadirai but she had never liked Pamela. She felt she gossiped too much.

"But would you be capable of doing that?" asked Judith.

"Of stealing somebody's husband? I wouldn't be the first person to do that would I?" Dadirai said before she and Pamela laughed loudly.

"No, no. Killing someone?"

The two women looked at Judith as if they had never seen her before. All of the saliva in Dadirai's mouth dried up. She turned to Pamela, silently beseeching her to respond.

"What's gotten into you? Are you looking to send someone off to the afterlife?" Pamela asked.

"No, of course not! I wasn't thinking right, sorry. All this talk of Valerie is making me a bit uncomfortable."

Dadirai gave Judith a sympathetic smile before rubbing her shoulder. "Don't mind me, I like to play detective."

"And you are very good at it too. Remember when you found that man who was cheating on you? You tracked him down and pointed a gun at the two of them in that Benz of his."

Dadirai recalled the image of a slender woman with the man she had once loved, their bodies against the car. She didn't appreciate Pamela bringing up the memory.

"That was just a moment of madness. I would never do that again. But our dear Valerie was ready to put a bullet between somebody's eyes."

Judith ran a finger across her chin.

"What are you saying now?" Pamela inquired.

"Valerie was sleeping with a gun under her pillow. She was frightened for her life."

Pamela scratched the acne on her forehead. The oil and dirt settled in her nail beds.

"State your case Detective Dadirai," said Pamela.

"She was scared that one of her business partners was going to come after her. I don't know if you met a man with dreadlocks around her house in the past few days. He called himself Dread."

Dadirai's companions shook their heads. She went into detail describing the tall man with thin dreadlocks, his round face, plump lips and wide-open eyes. The others still could not identify him.

"Valerie had lots of men around that house. Now tell us what is so special about him?" Pamela was impatient.

"It was a business partner not one of her collection of boyfriends." Dadirai looked around as if they were surrounded by strangers before she continued, "They were involved in diamonds trading."

"Diamonds?"

"Now I know you are lying to us," Pamela stood up, poised to leave.

"I'm not lying. You think her money was clean? I think she had a falling out with the man. He could have decided to slit that slender little throat of hers. If you see his face for yourselves you wouldn't even disagree. He is scarier than a baboon."

Pamela tried to stifle her laughter. She pushed the image from her head.

"How did our dear friend ever get involved with such a man?"

"She was a hustler that one! They must have met at one of those upmarket bars she liked to frequent."

Judith excused herself to go to the bathroom. When she returned, she announced that she was leaving.

"Are the stories becoming too frightening for you?" mocked Pamela.

"No, I'm just tired and I have to pick up a friend early tomorrow morning. We are going to church together."

Dadirai stood up to give her a hug.

"Travel safely tomorrow when you leave for Chivhu. As for Valerie, may her soul rest in peace and may justice prevail," this was Pamela to Dadirai before announcing her departure.

"You know what they say: *Chisi hachieri musi wacharimwa*," solemnised Judith.

"You are right. Thank you for your company tonight, ladies. I will let you know about the funeral arrangements when they are in place."

Judith took off in her box shaped car a few minutes later. Pamela stayed a bit longer before walking outs of the gate to meet her taxi driver. Dadirai accompanied her to the gate.

When Dadirai arrived back at her front door, the porch light
was shining.

A HEAD FULL OF DREAMS

Taurai carefully picked up the small pieces of gold from the muddy water. His wet blue shorts weighed him down as he walked towards dry land. He packed the gold into a green packet, then lay on the ground to let the sun dry his naked torso. His skin shone with each movement he made and it excited him to see the way the light bounced off him.

The smell of warm dust enfolded him under the midday sun that boiled the ground until it sizzled. A green fly landed on his large pink lips. He pushed it away lazily and opened his eyes. The sun temporarily blinded him. When his eyes recovered, he surveyed the scene of women and men who worked mechanically in the earthy water, separating the sand from the precious metal, their backs bent crookedly. Three women had tied their hair with rags and had bright coloured *zambias* around their waists. On trees that stood on the outskirts of the small yard were trousers, t-shirts and cloths hanging casually, seemingly spent by the dry heat. His crimson red t-shirt was easy to spot hanging off a dried branch that looked like it could give way at any moment. He slid on a pair of black trainers and his t-shirt. His tiny chest itched the moment it made contact with the fabric.

"Leaving already, boss?" asked one of the miners.

"Eh! I'm done for the day." He had not managed to collect a lot of gold that day but felt no need to tell the other miner.

"*Bho* boss! We'll see you tomorrow," said the miner as he wiped away a clump of mud from his forehead.

Taurai put the gold in his bag and walked back home, only stopping at a tuck shop to buy a loaf of stale bread. He arrived at his one roomed cottage in the late afternoon. A subtle earthy aroma filled the room. The bed was unmade.

Grey cement patches had begun creeping through the mint green walls. He had covered up some of the patches with pictures of women he had cut out of magazines.

He pulled one avocado from the two that were under the gas stove. He cut out the soft in-between of the bread and filled it with the creamy avocado. He sat on the bed and ate hungrily. When he was halfway through the delicacy, there was a knock on his door. Taurai jumped and covered the food with a plastic bag before he shoved it under the bed. He found a broken piece from a mirror in a corner and used it to adjust his short hair. He ran his right hand over his beard, the hair scratching his palm. There was another knock. This time the knock was harsh.

"Taurai?" Portia called out.

He immediately scrambled to remove the magazine pictures from the walls, which he carelessly stuffed in a cupboard before he went to open up the door.

Portia's braided hair was pulled back and tied with a beaded scrunchie. She looked especially beautiful. She was wearing a short, sleeveless floral dress. His smooth skin was the colour of dark wood.

"What took you so long? Were you sleeping?"

"No, I was just lying on the bed," his eyes twitched.

She slid past him and entered the room.

"Have you already finished work for the day?"

"It was a slow day today."

She sat at the foot on the bed, avoiding his mouldy pillow.

Taurai got onto the bed and sat close to her, his legs crossed. He ran a finger on Portia's knee and she instantly pulled away.

"You should move out of here. It smells." There was a stretched emphasis on the 'smells.'

"It's all I can afford for now, what do you want me to do? Buy a mansion with a pool and yard?"

"It wouldn't be so bad would it, Mr. Gold digger?"

She rested her back against the wall and took in a deep breath. Her shoulders relaxed and Taurai watched as her breasts heaved forward. Portia noted how his lips were parted as he ogled her for a few seconds.

"Don't look at me like that. When was the last time you called me?"

"You know how my phone is; the battery has been flat for a week now."

She scoffed, "That's no excuse."

Taurai lay on the bed, resting his head on the pillow. He tried to pull her towards him but she resisted.

"I don't like your behaviour."

"I looked for you at your house two days ago. Maybe if you let me talk to your siblings it would be easier for us. I would have whistled through the gate but that's old fashioned. *Muri vasikana vechimanje-manje ka imimi ana Portia.*"

She turned to face him. Slowly, she lowered herself onto the bed, bringing her face so close to Taurai's, she could feel his breath.

"I missed you," said Taurai.

"Rubbish! You didn't even bother to call or text."

"I'll be busy working for you *ka*? My sweet, my honey."

He caressed her back with his rough hands. Their legs were soon entangled. Portia brushed her lips against Taurai's before she kissed him. He undressed himself before he pulled off her dress urgently. He was now lying on top of her as he took each breath away with every rose kiss. His hands moved all over her like he was moulding her gently. When he was finally inside her, he was aggressive yet considerate, adjusting his movements to match her rhythm. She wanted to lie on a bed full of rose petals, with the sweet scent of candles around them, just like she read in the romance novels from the library.

Spent, they lay next to each other, taking ragged breaths. Taurai wanted her to say something – she usually did after they had made love – but she kept quiet. He could only hear her breathe on as she lay her head on his chest. She smelled like Camphor Cream.

"Aren't you going to say anything?"

"I have nothing to say." She opened her wet eyes and looked at him. What the eyes said frightened him. *I'm in love with you.*

"When are you going to buy your mansion Mr. Gold digger?"

"Soon. We're going to live in a big mansion in Harare. In Borrowdale," he remembered the name of the affluent neighbourhood he had once visited as a child visiting an aunt who worked as a domestic worker in one of the many mansions. "And I'll take you all over the world on my private jet. London, Paris, America. Everywhere my honey. Everywhere."

He kissed her once more, searching for the honey under her tongue.

"You say that yet you won't even marry me? You won't even look for me unless I look for you."

"Portia *iwe*. You know I love you. I think about you all the time. But I also have to make ends meet. I can't marry you now. Look at the place I'm living in."

"I have a few months before I graduate. And you know after I finish, I'm waiting for you to make the move."

They put their clothes back on. As Portia made her way to the door, Taurai told her he would call her that night. He watched as she walked away, her body swaying slowly in the hot air. He pulled the bread and avocado from under the bed and continued eating.

The room was becoming unbearably warmer as the day went by. Taurai stretched out on the bed, thinking of Portia and taking in the herbal smell she had left on his sheets. There was another knock on the door. Irritated at his imagination being disrupted, he shouted for the person to enter. Chitendo walked in.

"Ah Chichi! *Ndiwe?*"

Chitendo walked a few steps before jumping. When Taurai asked her what the problem was, she pointed at the condom on the floor. He picked it up and threw it into the dustbin.

"You should be ashamed of yourself Taurai!"

"It's only natural. Don't act as if you don't do it."

"I'm not talking about…" She took a look at him and exhaled. She handed him a packet of salted pumpkin seeds. The parcel was quickly packed away into the cupboard.

"So, who was it this time? That university girl of yours?" She deliberated for a moment, "…Portia?"

Taurai nodded.

"So, I guess you finally ended it with that girl of yours from the village?"

"No. Why should I?"

"Taurai! Your penis is going to fall off with these games you are playing!"

He laughed hard. He and Chitendo could speak to each other about anything.

"Are you and this Portia even serious?"

"One of us is serious."

Chitendo laughed heartily.

"What is she studying at the university by the way?"

"Psycho… physio…psy…something."

Chitendo laughed again. "I thought you would pick her to be your wife."

"Portia *akazvarwa*! But she isn't the one. She isn't going to be the queen to my castle."

"You boys! When we come here you treat us like queens but when you are bored with us, you spit us out like vomit. Anyways, when do you plan to buy your big mansion?"

"Soon. Very soon."

"That's not an answer." She sat on a rusted chair next to the gas stove.

"Greatness takes time, don't you know that? One day I'll host you at my mansion."

She opened the other packet of pumpkin seeds she had brought with her. She offered him some but he refused. Chitendo shrugged and began to eat, chewing loudly, Taurai thought the seeds might erode her teeth.

"Farai left for South Africa," he blurted out.

"That friend of yours that helped you at the mine?" asked Chitendo.

"Yes. He said he is going to be the next Michael Jackson."

"He can't even dance! I remember that stupid dance of his at his concert last week. Maybe he has a better chance of being Oliver Mtukudzi, he is brilliant on the guitar. When did he leave?"

"Last night. He left for Harare and said he would board the next bus to Mzanzi. So I'm going to be a millionaire, Farai is going to be the next Oliver Mtukudzi. What are you, Chitendo, going to be?"

"When you get to this age you see what life is about. Let dreams be dreams."

"You're only thirty, why can't you have dreams?"

"Who has the time? I have three children to take care of that my sister left me. I need to work, not dream."

A phone buzzed. Taurai plucked out a Nokia from under the pillow. He said a little prayer that it was not Portia. To his delight it was Mama Diamond. He told Chitendo that his client was on her way.

"Finally, I get to meet the notorious Mama Diamond."

"There is nothing much to see. She is a gangster woman from Harare."

Chitendo pictured a skinny woman in jeans, a t-shirt with the playboy bunny embossed on it and large sunglasses.

"I was serious Taurai, when do you plan to finally settle down?"

"In a year or two, by then I'm sure I should be on my feet."

***

A muddy, white BMW pulled up outside of the cottage. The two of them stepped outside to greet the new arrival. Chitendo was surprised to see a plump woman step outside of the car. An afro crowned the top of her apple-shaped head. She wore black jeans that matched her black leather jacket. Her eyes were hidden under dark sunglasses. She made her way towards the cottage and gave Taurai an embrace.

"How are you sonny?"

"I'm good mama. How was your drive?"

"Ah, these roads! You can't drive smoothly like the old days, you'll just be driving into pothole after pothole. And then the police! I would have arrived earlier but I was stopped over by the police. They found me with my quart between my thighs."

"You could have just given them money for a Coke or two."

"Your mother doesn't have any money sonny. Hopefully after I sell the gold, I can get something to pay my bills with." She paused and turned to Chitendo, "Hi darling!"

"Hi mama. How are you?"

"This is Chitendo. She is my friend," said Taurai, looking towards the ground.

"Oh, nice to meet you darling."

"Nice to meet you too mama."

Taurai rushed into the cottage to retrieve the gold while Mama Diamond and Chitendo awkwardly spoke about the weather. Mama Diamond was handed the rough metal in a cloth. She unwrapped it and frowned. She looked at him then looked at the gold again.

"I know. It has been a slow few weeks. I think the land is getting empty." Taurai shifted uncomfortably, averting his eyes from the big woman's.

"I last came here three weeks ago. And this is all you give me? *Usatambe neni iwe.*"

Taurai mumbled a few words under his breath.

"Or are you keeping some of it for yourself?"

"Of course not, you know I'm loyal."

She tilted her head up to the sky. Chitendo was disturbed by the oily lines around her neck.

"I hope that's true sonny because you know me."

"Of course mama! I would never betray you, never."

She handed him a thick wad of US dollar notes. He counted the money quickly. There was an extra ten dollars, but he did not tell her.

She folded the cloth and walked back to the car. She told him he would be hearing from him soon. The BMW sped into the distance as the two friends looked on.

"That mama of yours is a character." Chitendo had an expression of disgust on her face.

"She is a business partner. I don't care about her character."

"She scared me when she threatened you. What did she mean by 'you know me'?" Chitendo made a perfect imitation of Mama Diamond's squeaky voice. They were back in the room, Taurai now eating some of the pumpkin seeds.

"She told me once that her garden boy stole expensive clothes from her. When she found out she hired two men to beat him up and leave him naked on the streets. He packed his bags and never came back."

"Ah! You better hurry up and build that mansion of yours. Then you can get far away from people like your Mama Diamond."

"Chichi! You worry too much," he repeated. "Relax! Nothing will happen to me."

She stood, dusting her jean skirt with her arms.

"*Regai tiende zvedu*. I leave early tomorrow for Harare."

"Holiday?"

"Don't mock me! I need to buy a school uniform for Chenai."

Taurai was surprised to hear that the youngest of her nieces was already starting grade one.

He decided to leave for the city centre with her. They walked in silence for a distance.

"Why are you quiet?" asked Chitendo.

"Nothing. Just thinking of tomorrow."

"I hope you'll be safe from harm."

"I'll be safe from harm and closer to my dreams!"

She laughed. "I hope so. Well this is my turn. I'll see you when I come back."

Chitendo turned into a dusty road that led up to her house. Taurai stayed to wait for an omnibus. He didn't have to wait long before one came speeding along that had the words "KING OF ZIM" stickered onto the back. He decided to buy his mother a radio he had seen in town with the extra ten dollars Mama Diamond had given him.

HERE COMES MISTER WHITE

"They have a Benz?" Auntie Dot paused for a second, "Witchcraft *chete*!"

The woman who was putting rollers in her hair paused for Auntie Dot to stop shaking her head.

"No Auntie!" Fungai said to her aunt in a sour tone.

"Yes *muzukuru*! I bet you she has one of those snakes that vomit money for her. That's why she doesn't like people visiting her."

They were talking about Fungai's distant cousin who had offered to let Fungai's sister Shinga use her Mercedes Benz on her wedding day. Auntie Dot had had an argument in the past with the owner of the car over misused money which was never resolved. Auntie Dot was happy to let the animosity between them continue; it gave her the opportunity to gossip about someone without reservation. And there was no better place to spread gossip than the salon, the root of the grapevine. No topic was off limits and Auntie Dot took full advantage of that.

"Shinga has done wonders finding herself a white boy from the UK, maybe he can set you up with his brother."

"I'm not interested auntie."

"Why not Fungai? You're gorgeous! Look at those cheekbones of yours and that figure. People would kill to look like you," the bony girl who was styling Fungai's dreadlocks concurred.

"We have good genes in our family o," said Auntie Dot, attempting to imitate the way people spoke in Nigerian films.

"We used to say 'Mr White is always Mr Right,'" spat Auntie Dot. Everybody in the salon burst into laughter.

Fungai smiled as she looked down at the pretty picture of Cate Blanchet on the issue of *Woman & Home* magazine resting on her lap. Fungai tipped the hairdresser five dollars when she had finished. The skinny girl was bursting with gratitude and wished multiple blessings upon Fungai. As they left the salon, a woman with a ruffled afro passed them and asked whether her hair dresser was available.

Fungai drove while Auntie Dot wolfed down her fish and chips. She complained how greasy the fish was, how stale the potatoes were and that she was sure the server had picked a few of the chips. Their journey was a little under fifteen minutes. They found a white Mercedes Benz parked on the front lawn. Auntie Dot slapped the bonnet, her golden rings producing a glittery sound on contact.

"Nonsense!" she spat.

Shinga was trying on her wedding gown when Auntie Dot and Fungai entered the living room. The women in the room were singing and dancing, showering the soon to be bride with praise. She took in the adoration as humbly as she could.

"You look like an angel my daughter," said Shinga's mother, Mrs Hove.

Shinga thanked her mother. The other people in the room were Shinga's maid of honour, Precious and the wedding photographer capturing the memories on her tiny black camera.

Fungai tried to remember Edward's face. When Shinga had described him to her she had pictured a star from the American movies that she loved to watch with her father when she was younger; the chiselled, muscular leading man from action films that walked through fires and remained unharmed. When she finally saw him she was surprised to see a man who was not much taller than her sister, a stout man with silky red hair and a full beard that covered almost his whole face. His eyes were sleepy. Edward looked much older than her sister though he was only five years her senior. Fungai had brought this up one night when she was in conversation with Shinga and Auntie Dot.

"Some people age earlier than others," Shinga had defended her bridegroom.

"In a few years' time he will look old enough to be your *sekuru*!"

"That doesn't matter. *Murungu ndizvo*! Don't let anybody tell you otherwise Shinga," Auntie Dot had cheered, coughing out cigar smoke.

"You say it as if you speak from experience," Fungai had said inquisitively.

"Maybe I do!"

***

It had been all arranged. Shinga and Edward would be married then she would move with him to the UK in three months. They would be gone before Christmas. Fungai demanded that her sister send them a Christmas card, one with glitters and reindeers. Her sister would have a Christmas with snow and Christmas trees. She would have a stocking with her name hanging from the fireplace. They would prepare turkey and cranberry sauce for Edward's family. There would be no family visit to the farm. There would be no rice and chicken.

They were serving rice and chicken at the wedding though, with a host of other handsome looking dishes that no one could pronounce the names of. They specifically refused for *sadza* to be served. Though Edward had eaten up all the *sadza* that had been prepared for him one day, Shinga thought it would make his guests from outside the country feel uncomfortable. Fungai thought of the complaints that would come from the guests; complaints about the food, complaints about the décor, and complaints about being behind time. This was the order of the day at all the weddings that she had attended.

The pastor who was going to officiate the wedding arrived just as the wedding gown was being put back in its case.

"Is that Phantom yours?" Auntie Dot exclaimed, her jaw almost on the ground. She was referring to the grey Rolls-Royce the pastor had arrived in.

"Yes, all by the grace of God," the pastor said. Her expression was gentle but also showed irritation.

"*Nyasha shuwa*," Auntie Dot gazed at the vehicle.

Pastor Veronica had come to pray for Shinga before the wedding. After they had exchanged greetings, Shinga knelt in front of the pastor who placed her hands on Shinga's head and began to pray.

"Mighty Father, we come before you on this glorious day. We have been brought here by your daughter Shinga whom we speak a cascade of blessings upon! Bless her marriage oh Father God. Bless their children oh mighty God and may they be plentiful and rule over the nations. I pray for the blood of Jesus to break any foil or curse that may try to interfere with her marriage. I cast out any demon that has settled on her life! I vanquish any Satanic spirit that has harmed her in the past!"

She began to speak in tongues, some of her saliva settling on Shinga's glowing weave.

"Church, are we in agreement?" screamed Pastor Veronica.

"Amen," responded the others weakly.

"I said, church are we in agreement?" she repeated.

"Amen!" the response was stronger.

"Amen!" this was Auntie Dot in a mocking tone.

"Remember what I told you my daughter, as long as you become like the Proverbs 31 woman you will have everything you need to make your marriage successful. Never forget that," Pastor Veronica advised.

Fungai hated Proverbs 31. She had been hearing it since her time in Sunday school. It was touted as what they should aspire to become, the zenith of any woman's success.

Pastor Veronica concluded her prayer and was given a fruit cake as a gift before she left.

"How can your pastor afford such an expensive car?" Auntie Dot asked, as soon as the Rolls-Royce exited the gate.

"That's none of our business auntie," Shinga reprimanded.

"The congregation must know where their hard earned tithes are going. Or maybe she has snakes that cough up money. But you have nothing to worry about with Edward! These white boys' money is clean. He doesn't spend his time running around *kun'anga*."

The rest of the women in the room became silent.

"Has he finally bought a cow for your mother?" asked Auntie Dot

"Not yet." Edward had already been charged over fifty thousand dollars for Shinga's bride price.

"Then there isn't going to be a ceremony tomorrow, as long as *mombe youmai* hasn't been delivered."

"Most people are getting married without it. They will just pay for it later when they can afford to." Fungai defended her sister.

"These days people can even substitute it with something like a sewing machine," this was Precious.

"You children want to bend our culture, that's your problem!"

Shinga had already agreed with her mother that Edward could bring the *mombe youmai* later. They had not told Auntie Dot fearing she would object to the omission.

Auntie Dot pulled out her phone and dialled Edward's number. "Hello… Edward! How are you?" she went outside.

"That aunt of yours!" said Shinga's mother.

Auntie Dot came back after about five minutes.

"That boy has a sweet tongue, he can convince even the rain to stop falling," Auntie Dot was calmer now. "You should have asked him to give you a car in place of a cow though." She clapped her hands and giggled, believing she had said something humorous, her voice high pitched like a songbird.

"There is a woman I heard about who did that," said Mrs Hove, "Her husband had an accident with the car."

"It was probably just a common accident," said Precious.

"*Iwe*! Those are bad spirits speaking right there!" spat Auntie Dot.

"That is your answer to everything," Shinga accused.

When her father had died, Auntie Dot had said it was witchcraft because how could a man as successful as him succumb to death. Auntie Dot insisted that the witch was alive and still living among them and had to be dealt with.

"Did you hear that Edward is going to deliver his vows in Shona?" said Precious. Shinga gave her a sharp look, a look that could pierce through rocks with ease.

"*Hee?* I can't wait to see how people react when they hear that. *Ichava jambanja!*" Auntie Dot said.

"He has been learning Shona. Just yesterday we had a conversation where he didn't use a single English word," said Mrs Hove.

"That was between the two of you mum, imagine tomorrow in front of all those people," Fungai joined the conversation.

"It's going to be hilarious!" predicted Auntie Dot.

"I don't know why people would laugh at him for speaking in Shona." Shinga was irritated, "Nobody laughs when we speak in English no matter how many mistakes we make."

"That's because you are expected to speak in English if you want people's respect. Your fiancée speaking in Shona is just a joke. He doesn't need to prove anything to anybody," Mrs Hove chimed in.

"Your sister here said she's not interested in having Edward's brother for herself."

"Because I'm not ready for that yet auntie," Fungai said.

"Don't wait too long Fungai or else I'll take him," said Precious. Auntie Dot clapped her hands with glee.

"You'll never go wrong there!"

"Please! All men are the same!" this was Mrs Hove.

"No they're not, *varungu vari* romantic and thoughtful," Precious's voice sounded dreamy.

"And honest too!" Auntie Dot added, "Not like that good for nothing two timer that almost took everything I owned." She was referring to a younger man she had once dated who had promised to marry her only to discover that he had a wife and three children he had left in the village.

"Nobody is perfect in the world, you just have to love someone as they are," said Shinga.

"And love comes easier if the man is like yours!" said Auntie Dot.

A SISTER THING

Nyarai's sister-in-law, Rebecca, had found the job for her through an agency. Rebecca warned her against common mistakes that the house help could make such as burning clothes when she ironed, or eating too much food. And most importantly, she was to avoid having an affair with the man of the house because these things always came out. *Rina manyanga hariputirwe*, she had said. Rebecca joked that the chances of her getting into a relationship with Ruvimbo's husband were non-existent because he was never at the house.

"This should be an easy job. She doesn't have children and she is as good as single." Rebecca herself worked for a family that had five children, all of them under twelve years. "The woman I work for *anozvara semunhu anopenga*! She is going to have another baby soon I tell you."

Nyarai did not understand why Ruvimbo needed a house help when she did not work, but she was grateful for the opportunity and did not dwell on the matter. Since her husband lost his job at a furniture manufacturing company, he was now what Rebecca called a DDO – a daily drinking officer. He spent his days at the growth point and it was left to Nyarai to take care of their three children.

Ruvimbo gave Nyarai a quick tour of the house. It was a four bed-roomed estate in a suburb called Philadelphia. Her quarters were in a small cottage in the backyard. Ruvimbo encouraged her to make herself comfortable.

A list of her duties had been prepared, the tasks organised by days. As it turned out, she did not have much work to do around the house. She was required to cook, perform a thorough clean of the house fortnightly and tend to the garden once or twice a week. Nobody ever visited so there was never anything to clean. Ruvimbo spent most of her days watching television, reading novels or walking around the garden.

One afternoon, Ruvimbo approached Nyarai as she poured tomato juice into a beef stew. "I love that loud sizzle when tomatoes are thrown into the stew."

"Really? The noise always irritates me." Nyarai looked into the pot and thought she should have added more cooking oil. "Do you need something?"

"No, I just came to speak to you. Let me help you actually." Ruvimbo began to stir the broth. "So, tell me about yourself. I don't know anything about you, and we live in the same house."

Nyarai told her madam about her upbringing in the village, how she had been married off early and about her three children. They ended up eating together in the kitchen and talking for hours. They helped each other with the dishes and Nyarai bid Ruvimbo a restful night just as the clock edged toward eleven.

***

The only meals Nyarai had to prepare were breakfast and supper. Ruvimbo often had toast with beans during lunchtime. She was initially terrified because she had thought people who lived in fancy houses only ate exotic dishes but Ruvimbo turned out to be nothing like that. In the morning, she had mealie porridge and usually had *sadza* for supper that she liked to have with *matemba*, stewed okra or pumpkin leaves mixed with peanut butter. At times Ruvimbo would just come and sit in the kitchen as Nyarai cooked and ask her about her family life or listen to the radio with her while commenting on the stories.

Ruvimbo was invited by a friend of hers to a Pentecostal church one Sunday; her friend was getting baptised. She asked Nyarai to attend the service with her so she would be in the company of a familiar face. The two women sat together at the back of the church. When the preacher began speaking Ruvimbo struggled to pay attention to what he was saying. She looked beside her and saw a woman applying nail polish. The woman could feel her stare.

"I couldn't concentrate so I decided to do some personal grooming."

Ruvimbo nudged Nyarai showing her the spectacle.

"When she's done, I'm going to ask to use the nail polish too!" said Ruvimbo.

Nyarai laughed. Nobody could hear her over the shouting and loud drumming in the church.

Nyarai came to understand there were times when Ruvimbo was not to be interrupted. Those were when she watched *The Young and the Restless* in the morning and *The Bold and the beautiful* in the late afternoon. Nyarai tried to watch them but she simply could not follow how fast the characters spoke. She instead watched South African shows after supper, relating to the traditional lives of the people in *Muvhango* and finding delight in the over sensationalised *Rhythm City*.

Nyarai met Rugare one afternoon when she had the day off. She was leaving Nyarai's house when she saw a woman with a white scarf tied around her head and a child on her back.

"*Makadii?*" asked Nyarai.

"I'm well thanks, how are you?"

"I am great. Is that your baby?"

"Ah! As beautiful as I am, do you think I would have such an ugly child?"

Rugare explained that the child belonged to her employers. She was on her way to church.

"So you're Mrs Moyo's new house help?" asked Rugare.

"Yes."

"Have you met her husband yet?"

"No, I haven't."

"He is probably *ku*small house," suggested Rugare.

"Small house? Do you mean they own a smaller house?"

"No! His second wife," said Rugare amazed at Nyarai's naivety, "We used to think she was the second wife but as it turns out she is the first wife."

It was not that Nyarai was unfamiliar with the concept of polygamy; her own grandfather had married twenty-two wives. But it seemed strange to her because these people lived in large houses in the city and back in her village polygamy was very common.

"That's just how men are. When my husband moved to Cape Town he married another woman. He hasn't paid her bride price yet though."

Ruvimbo's husband finally made an appearance four months after Nyarai had started her job. He was a tall dark-skinned man with very little to say to Nyarai. His presence cast a shadow on the relationship that had been growing between the two women. He seemed to take up the whole space and left very little room for light and laughter in the house. Ruvimbo and Mr Moyo did not speak very much; Ruvimbo often left him in the lounge as he watched European football matches on TV. She would busy herself with movies in her bedroom or go out with her friends. Nyarai was grateful when Mr Moyo left after his weekend visit.

She visited Rugare's workplace that afternoon. It was a large five-bedroomed house that was painted an odd shade of maroon. In the back was a gorgeous garden and an oval shaped swimming pool. Rugare was alone with the baby.

"He is such a scary man!"

"I've only ever seen him once driving down the street, but I could tell he is not very nice," said Rugare.

When they were tired of gossip, Rugare asked Nyarai to follow her to the master bedroom. The bedroom seemed unlived in with the shiny wooden floors, the antic Elizabethan vanity and the large king-sized bed covered in white linen. Rugare swung open the walk-through closet and grinned at her friend. She took off her clothes and pulled out a sequined gown before trying it on. When she was done she looked at herself in the mirror. She went on to try all the other clothes, wigs, scarves and high heeled shoes she looked like she would tumble out of. Nyarai lay on the bed and took pictures.

"I don't have much work to do so let me enjoy my free time." When Rugare was done, she picked out a few of the clothes and took them to her bedroom.

"Won't your madam notice?"

"I'll just say they went missing at the dry cleaners. Besides, she doesn't even wear these."

That evening, after Nyarai had finished doing the dishes, Ruvimbo called her up to her bedroom. The bed was heaped with clothes.

"You can take whatever you like from there?" said Ruvimbo pointing at the clothes.

"Serious madam?"

Ruvimbo nodded. "I wanted to do it earlier but I waited for Mr Moyo to leave first."

Nyarai started to pick through the clothes and carry them to her room. Dozens of sparkly shirts and flowy dresses now belonged to her. She texted Rugare that she had the best madam on the street.

Nyarai would send money and groceries to her mother via a bus that went to their village every fortnight. One day, Rugare suggested Nyarai help her open a clothes stall at a nearby flea market. They would use Rugare's stolen clothes and the clothes Nyarai was given as a start. Then they would use their profits to order clothes from Mozambique. Nyarai liked the idea and they set up the shop one Saturday afternoon when both of them were off duty.

Nyarai moved into the main house at the insistence of Ruvimbo. As they were carrying Nyarai's belongings into the bedroom downstairs, Ruvimbo noticed most of the clothes that she had given Nyarai were missing.

"I don't see the clothes I gave you?"

"I sold them for extra money with my friend," answered a sheepish Nyarai.

"But they were a gift! If you needed more money you should have told me. How could you sell them?"

That night Ruvimbo did not leave her bedroom for supper and in the morning she refused to have breakfast. At lunchtime, Nyarai visited Rugare and told her about the incident.

"When these people fight with their husbands, they take it out on us. When my madam does that to me, I just scrub the toilet with her toothbrush."

Nyarai and Rugare continued to operate their clothes stall but the money they earned from it was nothing compared to Nyarai's weekly wage. Her wages were able to afford her three children's school fees and send them groceries every other week. She began thinking of saving some of the money for when her children started high school. She wanted them to attend boarding schools.

For Christmas, Nyarai was given two weeks off. She decided to buy Ruvimbo a gift before she left. She got her a sequined scarf which was received gratefully. Nyarai asked her employer what she would do for Christmas. Ruvimbo said she was going to celebrate alone.

Nyarai arrived at her village on Christmas eve to find her children playing outside of their small house. When they recognised her from a distance, they sped towards her and embraced her. They stained her floral dress but she did not mind. The children reported that their father had been away for three days, drinking at the local shops. On Christmas morning a Jeep sped up to the house and out jumped Ruvimbo. The back seat was filled with canned foods, clothes and books.

"You said you wanted a big Christmas. I hope that this can make it bigger!"

The children approached Ruvimbo's car with hesitation.

"I don't bite!" joked Ruvimbo handing the children the parcels. Nyarai could tell that her children warmed up to Ruvimbo. They turned on the radio and danced to old school music. Nyarai was initially nervous to dance in front of her madam. It was Ruvimbo who danced unapologetically that encouraged the rest of the group to join in. The children giggled at how unapologetically Ruvimbo danced.

"We should have a prize for the best dancer," Ruvimbo was breathless, "Does anyone think they can beat me?"

"I can try," declared Nyarai. Nyarai proved to be more flexible than Ruvimbo as she swished around effortlessly to the glossy guitar riffs and banging drums.

"Yes Mama! Yes!" the children cheered on. The two women decided to call it a tie and they all agreed they were hungry. They opened up the cans, uncorked the bottles and had a hearty meal. Ruvimbo seemed genuinely interested in the children's schooling and their social lives. They narrated stories about her newest friend or the teacher they sorely disliked.

Ruvimbo spent the whole day with Nyarai's family, celebrating with them and only decided to leave when the sun was setting.

Nyarai saw her husband only once during her two weeks stay at the village. Her children told her that he barely came around the house since she left. He spent his nights at the growth point.

***

Derek first visited Ruvimbo a week after New Year's. He looked much younger than Ruvimbo, and Nyarai thought that he might be Ruvimbo's brother. There was a marked change in Ruvimbo when the guest arrived. She wore a different perfume and her voice took on an uncharacteristic high-pitched coo. Nyarai listened in on their conversations while she was in the kitchen. She quickly realised the two were having an affair.

Derek ended up spending the night to Nyarai's surprise. When she woke up to make breakfast, Ruvimbo was already dicing fruits in a bowl. She told Nyarai not to worry about preparing breakfast. Nyarai was uncomfortable with Derek's presence and avoided him as much as she could. It was finally Derek that approached Nyarai as she was watering the potted plants.

"Are you the one who planted these?"

"No."

"These flowers don't need that much water and they prefer being kept in partial sunlight. Let me help you."

He carried the potted plants to an area close to the garage.

"Give them three weeks and you'll see how beautiful they will come out."

"Thank you, sir."

They then went to the front yard where he started fishing out dead leaves from the pool. She had told him that she would do it but he insisted.

"I hope you are being nice to Nyarai. I can't afford to lose her." Ruvimbo's voice came from behind them.

"I would never do that to her! Such a nice woman."

Nyarai was amazed by this man who seemed so at ease with everything he did, this man who did not take himself too seriously. Derek spent a total of three nights and left.

"Three nights Rugare! Three!"

"She is lucky her husband doesn't know. A man I know beat his wife when he found out she was cheating on him. Then he forced her to go to the mountain to repent. She fainted on her way to the mountaintop and died."

"Perhaps I should just hint at her to stop it."

"*Iwe! Unopenga?* She is your madam. So what if she has a boyfriend over? *Zvisiye!*"

Ruvimbo was in festive spirits one afternoon and she couldn't stop giggling as she spoke to Nyarai.

"Why are you so happy?" Nyarai asked.

"Derek is coming over tonight. I was thinking of making something special for him to eat. I've printed out a chicken recipe."

"It's okay." Nyarai tried to hide her discomfort at the news. They prepared the food together before Nyarai retired to her bedroom.

The next morning, she found Ruvimbo sleeping on the living room couch, still dressed in yesterday's clothes. The dinner table was still set. Nyarai woke her up.

"He didn't come last night." She was still sleepy.

"Sorry I guess," said Nyarai indifferently.

"Guess?"

"Maybe it was for the best. He isn't your husband after all."

"You wouldn't be saying that if you knew him the way I do."

"He isn't yours, madam!"

Ruvimbo stood up and took a good glance at the woman in front of her.

"Do you still want to work here?"

"I'll think about it."

Nyarai considered what would happen to her if she lost her job. Her main worry was her children. She had been able to afford them some degree of comfort with the money that she earned from working for Ruvimbo, a luxury that she knew most maids could not afford. In the instance that she did manage to keep her job, she did not know if she could continue having Derek around as if what Ruvimbo was doing was honourable.

It was not Nyarai but Rugare who lost their job. Rugare was fired one Sunday morning. Her employer simply told her to move her things and to leave the house. Her life for the past five years was packed in a single black suitcase.

"I think they found out that I was stealing from them."

"Did you think you weren't going to be caught?"

"Don't act as if you did not benefit from the things I stole. I guess we can continue selling clothes at the flea market while I look for another job."

"As a maid?"

"What else can I do?"

Rugare never showed up at the flea market. She no longer responded to Nyarai's text messages. Rugare had been the more business savvy of the two and without her, their stall was finally closed down.

Even though they were not on speaking terms, Ruvimbo noticed that something was wrong with Nyarai.

"What's the matter?"

"My husband is very sick. They tell me it's his liver. My oldest daughter has even stopped going to school so she can take care of him."

"How long has this been going on?"

"A little over a month. My children knew that if I heard it I would have gone there and left this job."

Ruvimbo offered her a week off to visit her family and even offered to drive her. Nyarai accepted the time off but decided to take the bus home.

Nyarai let go of her job as a maid. She decided she would return home to take care of her husband full time.

"I could never do that," said Ruvimbo, "you are brave."

"If I take care of my husband, my oldest daughter can return to school. I have to give my children an opportunity to do better than I did."

"It's the end of something for the both of us I guess. Mr Moyo has told me to leave this house. He is moving in with his other wife and children."

MOMENTS IN THE PRIVATE ROOM

Teveraishe's body was discovered in the bottle store that was opposite his family's tuck shop. Detective Solomon is the one who finally took a closer look and found the man had been strangled.

The owners of the bottle store argued that they had nothing to do with the murder. They said they had closed shop a little after three in the morning. They had had to chase out a few drunken men, but had not seen Teveraishe among the crowd. They had even told the detective that they were certain Teveraishe had not come to have a drink the previous night.

"I always remember whoever comes here, *always*," said the bartender. She would snake her legs around most of the customer's waists when she wanted a few extra dollars.

When it was discovered that the lock in front of the bar's entrance had been broken, Solomon dropped any suspicion of the bottle store owners being involved in the murder. The detective arrived at Teveraishe's house late afternoon. Teveraishe's mother, Jocelyn, was sitting by the veranda, panting heavily, trying to form a clear sentence but failing each time. Her husband Aaron was in the living room, the television set humming away.

Solomon spoke to Jocelyn first. The woman had calmed down a little by the time she sat next to the handsome detective. She told him that she and Aaron had been at home the whole night. Solomon asked her if she knew anybody that might try to harm Teveraishe. The woman said she could not think of anybody who might try to kill her son. Throughout their conversation, Jocelyn would not make eye contact with him and some of her words were inaudible. He had to keep asking her to repeat herself in the hope of scratching at the core of any information she had.

Aaron was more reliable than his wife; he was forthcoming with the detective, telling him that their son worked in the tuck shop that was opposite the bottle store where his body was discovered. He had worked there for nearly fifteen years. He would occasionally have a drink or two at the bottle store after his shifts. Detective Solomon decided that was the best he could do on this day before making his way home.

Solomon found a plate filled with ox-tail and *sadza* on the kitchen counter. He had no appetite and left the food untouched. Inside the bedroom, he found his wife Talent already tucked into bed. He ran his hands across her figure perfectly outlined by the thin duvet.

"What are you doing?"

"I missed you," he said as he began rubbing her waist.

"Let me go."

"Please." It was a whisper. He kissed her neck.

"Let go, it won't help for anything," she said.

That night, he slept with his back towards his wife.

***

Detective Solomon decided to attend Teveraishe's funeral. He thought it would be good to listen in on the attendant's conversations. Jocelyn and Aaron's house was an hour away from his own and he arrived while the white casket was being carried into the house. Solomon stood at a distance, making himself as inconspicuous as he could. He was starting to feel that he had wasted his time coming. It was not until he had heard about Keresenziya that he found a reason to stay longer.

Keresenziya was Teveraishe's sister. She was a touring actress who had returned home a week earlier from South Africa. The detective approached her.

"My brother's name was Teveraishe. He did exactly what his name commanded; follow the Lord. That's if God wants him in his kingdom."

She told him that she had arrived from performing a play in Johannesburg recently and she had spent the night with a friend the night her brother was killed. She was working on a movie with a script being redone.

"It's going to be my first movie! I'll buy you tickets when it comes out. If you solve this mystery."

"I intend to," said the detective.

"Can you imagine this is going to be my first film? I'm almost thirty, you know? I should have won an Oscar by now. Have you seen that black actress who was nominated this year, Marianne Jean-Baptiste? I could have played her part with ease. I kind of look like her don't you think?"

Solomon did not know who the actress was.

***

When he went back to Jocelyn and Aaron's house, he found Keresenziya was the only one there. He could hear her voice as he arrived by the gate. She was running over her lines for the movie. The most outstanding possession that he believed Keresenziya had was her voice. It was the kind of voice that brought people to deep comfort in churches.

Keresenziya told him Jocelyn had gone to the hospital with Aaron to get her eyes checked.

"Have you come to bother us more with your tedious questions?"

"I have work to do. I have to find out what happened to your brother."

"I don't know if there is any other way we can help you. He lived and died."

"Tell me about your brother, did he have any enemies?"

"I don't know."

"Was he involved in any illegal activities that you knew of?"

"No."

"Anything important you think I should know?"

She rolled her eyes. "Look detective, why don't you go around digging in rubbish bins for evidence. My brother and I weren't close ever since I started touring. I don't know what he was up to. So why don't you just leave."

"I'd prefer staying." He was surprised he had said that, "Never mind! I'll find my way out."

"Feel free to come back any time," she teased him.

Solomon was stopped by a woman wearing an Adidas t-shirt as he left the house.

"Excuse me, are you working on Teveraishe's case?"

"Yes ma'am."

"There is something you might want to know."

"Tell me."

"Jocelyn acts as if she is innocent, but I can tell you, when it gets dark she is running around going to traditional healers. I'm sure Teveraishe's death has a more supernatural connection. *Chivanhu chaicho!*"

She wrote down the name of a traditional healer and his contact details on a piece of paper. She had referred Jocelyn to the traditional healer earlier last year.

"The healer encourages blood sacrifices," said the woman. "Have you made any sacrifices yourself?"

"Don't ask too much."

***

The traditional healer's house was a one bedroomed home on the western tip of Harare. The living room had been converted into his workspace. The floor was dusty. The healer sat on a wooden stool while a mat was laid in front for his clients. Detective Solomon found himself sitting on the mat. He first lied to the healer.

"Five years without a child? And you say your uncle also died without a child? *Ngozi*! *Ngozi chaiyo*!"

Solomon was handed a bottle filled with twigs and told to wash in it every night at the exact same time for six weeks. This was how he would remove any bad spirit that might be hovering over him. After this was done, he pulled out a wad of bills from his pocket and handed them to the healer.

"This is more than my asking price," said the healer as he flipped through the notes.

"I thought a few extra dollars would help me out with some information I need."

"What do you want to know *muzukuru*?"

"Your client Jocelyn, I'd like to know about her."

***

Detective Solomon went to Teveraishe's house after he had finished with the traditional healer. He found Jocelyn inside.

"I don't know what else I can tell you about our son. I don't know if he had any friends. Whenever he was here, he barely spoke about his friends or work. That's if he slept here at all."

"There was another place he was spending the night?" asked Solomon.

"Behind the tuck shop that he ran, there is a bedroom that we furnished for late nights but he spent most of his nights there… even after it was burnt down."

"The room was burnt down?"

"The place caught on fire while he was sleeping." She paused, "He barely escaped with his life. We still don't know what caused the fire."

"And he continued to sleep there?"

"He swept the ashes aside and continued sleeping there more than he did here." She was tired from speaking, "We are fixing the place up though. Keresenziya said she'd be there this afternoon painting the walls."

Keresenziya was painting the back room of the tuck shop when Solomon arrived. She was using a pale-yellow paint.

"Why are you here? I told you I have nothing to contribute to your investigation."

"I doubt that."

She dipped the paint brush and made swift movements across the wall. "I'm not saying anything detective. So either crawl back home or you can watch me do my work."

"Then I'll watch you paint."

He sat down and watched her paint across the wall. Her body stretched out gracefully like a butterfly with each movement. He had to return to the office so he reluctantly stood up.

"I'm not done yet."

"I'll return, don't worry."

Solomon returned in the early evening. Keresenziya was going through her script.

"You're later than I expected," said the actress as she led her companion into the room.

"What matters is I'm here isn't it?"

They hastily undressed each other and lay on the mattress. Solomon took control, thrusting inside her gently, kissing the contours of her smooth figure. Running a marathon across her body slowly.

"I told you to pull out!" she said. He hadn't heard her say so.

"Don't worry about it, nothing will happen."

"I'm not meant to be anybody's mother."

He knew this was not a way to coax information out of her. He had wanted to be around her as much as she had needed someone to keep her company, somebody to help scare away the ghosts that lived in the room. When she was certain of the emptiness of the ghouls, she led him out into the darkness. He arrived home in the early morning.

***

Nothing new was being uncovered about the case on Teveraishe's death. He prayed it would stay that way. Detective Solomon had become used to visiting Keresenziya in their private room. He had become comfortable sitting on the floor of the room which still smelt like fresh paint. She would light two candles as they ate dinner together. She would tell him that it was nothing romantic but only because the electrical wires were still broken. Solomon's wife was indifferent when he returned home. He would often find his supper wrapped up in plastic and sitting on the kitchen counter back at his house.

Finally, a man named Lance was arrested for Teveraishe's murder. The family was informed about it in the early morning and Jocelyn was taken away as an accomplice to the crime. Keresenziya cried to Solomon when he arrived at the tuck shop.

"They arrested my mother!" She was erratic, "They took her away in chains! She's an innocent old woman!"

Lance had come forth in a manic fit to report that he was hired to commit the murder by Jocelyn.

"They can't keep her in that prison forever can they? She couldn't have done it!" the actress said to her companion.

"Yes they can and you want to know why?" Solomon paused shortly, "She went to a traditional healer asking for medicine that would kill your brother. They have reason to believe that she wanted him dead. Don't ask me how I know that."

"My brother was strangled, not bewitched."

"He was strangled by a man who was under your mother's instruction."

"My instruction! Now help me get my mother out of prison please!"

He did not want the full picture but Keresenziya decided to give it to him anyway.

Keresenziya was the one who had set the back room on fire. She had taken five years of her brother's abuse. He told her that it was how she was going to become a woman so she had to comply with his visits to her bedroom. She had gone to South Africa to run away from him. She made every effort to avoid her brother whenever she came home.

One night, she was at home with her mother when she was told that Jocelyn was now Teveraishe's victim. The mother had become a successor to her daughter.

"I knew what he did to you," Jocelyn confessed one day to her daughter.

"And you decided to do nothing," said Keresenziya, "But I am going to do something."

Finding someone to kill her brother was easier than she had thought it would be. She asked around for someone who would be willing to do *anything*. The man was a poacher named Lance and he took the job without any hesitation. Keresenziya was the last person to receive the news about her brother's death. She made sure that she exaggerated her displeasure over her brother's passing, shouting as loudly as she could and going into a flight of thought whenever anybody spoke to her about it. They agreed that should they be caught, they would blame the crime on Jocelyn because they thought that the older woman would be given a lenient sentence.

"I won't say that my mother is innocent, she probably should have done something about what happened to me. But she shouldn't be in prison," said Keresenziya.

Solomon began to leave the room.

"Where do you think you are going? Spend the night."

"You are asking me to spend the night?"

She realised that this was the first time she had asked him for anything. She commanded him all of the time. He left.

***

The front door at Solomon's house did not unlock. He walked round the house to his bedroom window.

"Talent, the door won't open," he said while knocking on the window.

"I know."

"Let me in!"

"Go back where you came from Solomon," she replied, "And don't come back."

When Solomon arrived at Keresenziya's room, the front door was ajar. He opened it slowing and found her asleep on the floor. He slid next to her cosily.

"You should have slept on the front mat," she said.

"And yet you kept the door open for me."

"I kept it open to let in some fresh air."

"So she says," he retorted, "I think I'll look for a new line of work after I've helped get your mother out of prison."

STRANGE THINGS

Mazvita noticed something was wrong with the Pussycat dolls the same time she noticed something was wrong with Susan. Like other fans, she noticed that Nicole Scherzinger seemed to be the only person who sang lead for the Pussycat dolls and as for Susan, she was pregnant.

Of course the concept of pregnancy was nothing foreign to Mazvita. She was in her mid-teens and had already witnessed several pregnancies. Her mother had had three children after her. She had also seen the pregnancies of her aunts. The closest pregnancy was her cousin Yemurai's. Mavita was the first person that Yemurai had told about the baby. She was three months pregnant by then and Mazvita caressed her belly, trying to imagine how the little person would look when they were born. In the end, Yemurai lost the pregnancy at four months. Mazvita however, thought it was her parents who had forced the girl to terminate the pregnancy.

What was strange about Susan's pregnancy was that Susan was crippled. Mazvita simply could not fathom the idea of Susan having sex. Both of Susan's legs had been amputated and she spent most of her days sitting in a wheelchair outside a shop that sold makeup and perfumes. What had attracted Mazvita to the shop was the French style architecture. Mazvita decided to buy a makeup kit one afternoon after school and that is how she met Susan.

"I don't know if you need that. You are beautiful as you are." Those had been Susan's first words to her.

She was the first person to tell Mazvita she was beautiful and there was an instant connection between the two. Mazvita became one of the people that would regularly contribute to Susan's plate, often dropping in dollar bills that she had lying around in her satchel. In gratitude, Susan often offered words of encouragement to Mazvita to stay in school and to always give her best. It was from these conversations that Mazvita began to feel guilty about spending money on superficial things such as makeup when she could be using it on things that had 'meaning'. Eventually she stopped buying pretty things from the shop and would only pass by it to see Susan with her large smile; a smile whose warmth battled the sun's.

Mazvita's mother was a youth mentor at her church. Her favourite topic to lecture on was sexuality; her eyes seemed to brighten up when she talked about it as if she were a five-year-old who had been given sweets. She sometimes left condoms on Mazvita's nightstand. Mazvita would take them and give them to her friends, having no use for them herself. When she saw Susan's baby bump, she wondered whether she should have offered her some of the condoms.

It was not until someone told her that people slept with disabled people so they could release themselves of curses or evil spells that they had on them, that Susan's pregnancy became less of a shock. She agonised over whether this was the case with Susan; whether her friend was carrying the Devil's child.

Susan finally told Mazvita about her pregnancy herself.

"My king and I are expecting this little one in a few months. I could use every cent I can get."

"You're married?" it came out as a whisper.

"Who said you have to be married to have a child?" Mazvita stole a quick glance at Susan and looked away, but not before her friend had noticed. "Disabled people can have sex you know?"

One afternoon Mazvita went to see Susan after school but she was not there. She could not ask the people from the make-up shop, they were probably happy that Susan had left. Mazvita bought makeup for the first time in a while. She wondered how she would look when she applied it.

STILL HAVE TONIGHT

It was Nelson who told Njekwa that Sanyambe would be returning to Southern Rhodesia by the end of the year. Njekwa was not sure how to feel about the news. It was an afternoon in their parents' house, Njekwa was separating peas into a pot while her brother was speaking joyously to their parents. Nelson had arrived in Southern Rhodesia from Zambia a few hours ago. He looked different; certain flowers had bloomed in him and others had died.

"Don't you have anything to say? I said Sanyambe is coming back at the end of the year," said Nelson.

"I heard you *Va*Mandela," this was Njekwa, with stings in her words.

"One thing I will never miss about this place is people always calling me Mandela. I'm nothing like him," said Nelson.

"Coming from the boy who decided to return to his father's land when it gained independence," said their mother Mrs Phiri. "I'm sure your patriotism will make the two of you great friends."

Nelson had moved to Lusaka in 1965, a year after Zambia gained independence from the United Kingdom. Their father, Mr Phiri, had moved to Southern Rhodesia to find work and had stayed there ever since. He made sure he stamped his heritage on his youngest child Njekwa, a name which meant 'cause of laughter'. Their middle sister Frances was in Zambia studying towards her masters. She had promised to return when she was finished with her studies.

"You should come back with me. Unless you want to continue living under the white man."

"She'll never move. What's the point, she's doing very well here." This was Mr Phiri.

"Or maybe she won't leave because I told her that her boyfriend is coming back."

Njekwa made an ugly face at her brother before going to the kitchen to put the peas into the boiling water.

It was not until later that evening that memories of Sanyambe played in her mind. He would finally return from university in the United Kingdom. Not for her though; he probably would have outgrown her.

***

Nancy was the Indian who lived next door to Njekwa and she was also her workmate. The two went to work together. This was helpful to Njekwa who had recently moved into her own place. She was still trying to find her footing living on her own and appreciated Nancy's help. Nancy worked in the administration department for the psychology clinic that Njekwa worked in.

This morning, Nancy was particularly talkative. Her main focus was on the continued bush war which was taking place around the country. She expressed her terror that it may persist for a long time.

"It might not be a bad idea to take up your brother's offer to move to Zambia, Jay." Njekwa allowed Nancy to call her Jay because it was difficult for her friend to pronounce the stamp her father had placed on her.

"I'm comfortable here. We can only wait and see what will happen."

"Most likely it will turn out bad."

Njekwa knew that Nancy would begin to speak about her family's eviction from Uganda a few years earlier. Whenever Nancy spoke about the incident, she would break into tears.

"We left everything, everything Jay! Can you imagine that?" She would repeat the phrase like morning birds singing.

"Do you mind if we pass by the market when we go back home today?" asked Njekwa.

"Of course not!"

"I want to pick up fresh flowers for my flat."

"Are we finally having Charles over for dinner?" Nancy teased.

"Oh hush!" said Njekwa.

Charles, the tall Nigerian. Charles the dark-skinned statue. Charles with the spectacles. Charles who could never produce a proper sentence whenever he spoke to Njekwa. He had been pursuing her since she moved into her flat. He helped her to move boxes into the empty room. When they had finished, he offered her coconut rice and curried chicken. She apologised politely saying she did not want to eat, she just wanted to go to sleep.

That night she met Charles arriving home. Nancy snuck away from them to give them time to speak.

"Hello Njekwa," he said shyly, "Those are beautiful flowers."

"Thank you."

"I'll buy a bouquet for you one day, bigger than that one." Charles spoke with a deep Nigerian accent but very softly.

"So how is work at the university?" asked Njekwa.

"Challenging, but I am enjoying it."

"I'm glad to hear that!" she walked towards her flat, "Have a goodnight, Charles."

The man simply waved.

That night Njekwa allowed herself to think about Sanyambe properly, not the brief thoughts of him she had had in the past few days. She had last seen him what seemed to be very long ago, when she was nineteen. His family was Zambian by descent; his father worked for the railroad while his mother was a homemaker. He had four other siblings but he was often alone.

When she was ten years old Sanyambe had walked her home on a rainy day. Njekwa's siblings from then onwards called her Sanyambe's girlfriend. It wasn't until she was fifteen when they finally became a couple. They hid in empty allies and quiet bushes, but both of their families knew that they were together.

The next evening when Nancy and Njekwa came back home they met Charles coming out of his flat.

"Something tells me he is now stalking us," said Njekwa.

"Stalking you, Jay. He won't even look at me," said Nancy pulling out the groceries from her Peugeot 403 saloon. "Go and talk to your man! I'll get started on supper alone. You can join me later."

Charles towered over Njekwa, auspiciously drawing her attention.

"You look good today."

"Thank you," Njekwa said shyly, "Are you off somewhere?"

"I'm going to get a drink." Whiskey was his drink. "Or if you'd like we can go together or we can stay here for the night?"

"I won't be able to…"

"You can be an honest critic of my *nkwobi*. It's a delicacy in Nigeria. Of course I don't make it like my mother used to but I think I'm close. But my jollof rice is close to perfection."

"Thanks, but no thanks, tonight I'm going over to Nancy's. Another time."

"Just let me know whenever you can make it. I'll be prepared."

The front door to Nancy's was open. Nancy was wrapping a pink apron around her tiny waist.

"And?"

"He is going to get stupid drunk from what I see."

"Come on Jay! Give the man a chance. I don't see a reason why you wouldn't want to be with him. Unless perhaps there is someone else."

"No, of course not!"

"Good. Then I'm expecting to hear about your date with the Nigerian prince soon."

Njekwa struggled to finish her food.

That night she knocked on Charles's door.

"Njekwa! What can I do for you?"

"I'll be coming for dinner tomorrow." She began to walk towards her flat.

"Okay, but…"

"That is all for tonight."

***

Charles' flat was a work in progress. There were paint cans in one corner. Boxes of clothes were placed around the living room, on the floor, on the sofas. Njekwa was sitting at the dinner table as Charles spoke to her from the kitchen. Pinot noir was a fine complement to her jollof rice while she found cold water best with the *nkwobi*.

"The flavours! Isn't it too intense with the whiskey?" Njekwa asked her companion.

"I'm now used to it."

"The flavours are so strong!"

A few boxes were removed from the sofas. Charles turned on the radio and spoke to Njekwa.

"Do you enjoy teaching here?"

"It is fine, but the students are a bit of a challenge. It's quite hard to keep up with them."

"Why not return to Nigeria?" She later thought that she did not phrase the question properly.

"No! Not there!" This was the first time during the day he was dismayed. "Are you sure you don't want something to drink? There is plenty in the fridge?"

"You want me to drink so I don't make it home, right?"

"Your home is just next door, it would never be a problem for you."

"That's if you want me to go home."

It was their bodies that took over, not their minds. They wanted to feel every moment and hold the moon in place for as long as they could. Njekwa looked into his eyes, searching for something abstract. It was undefined but she knew that when she found it, he would know. She spent the night with him then. When morning came, she reluctantly went back to her flat in preparation for work.

It was shortly after Nelson left when Nancy received the news that her own brother had died in India. Nancy left for India immediately. Nancy left her keys with Njekwa, asking her to open her windows whenever she had the chance. The void that Nancy left was filled by Charles.

Her days were filled with the two of them meeting for dinners at each other's homes. He was able to fulfil a space she never knew was empty. His food was tasty though he complained it did not have the authentic taste that he wanted it to have. Whenever it was her turn to cook, she felt as if she was preparing a dish for royalty. Each recipe, each direction, each seasoning was treated with great precision. Charles finally revealed to her that he had escaped from Nigeria in 1969. He had lived in the newly formed country Biafra. Charles was able to escape from Biafra into Cameroon and from there, he found his way into Southern Rhodesia. He said it was because they spoke English there. His sister had been raped during the war and ran off into the forest one day; they never saw her again. His mother had died from malnutrition. There was nothing left in Nigeria for him.

Charles favoured his soul music. The tantalising timbre of James Brown's voice was their house guest almost every day. The Jackson five also frequently visited them. Njekwa found their music cartoonish. Whenever The Supremes's "Stop in the name of love" played on the radio, Charles picked Njekwa up and danced with her. It was one early evening when Charles was sweeping Njekwa across the floor to the song when she finally pulled away from him.

"I will never understand what you like about this stuff," she said.

"This is good music."

"Do you really want to hear good music?" Njekwa asked. Charles nodded. They took his car to Salisbury Township Recreation Hall. There was a jazz band playing that night led by a singer with a silky voice. The members were smartly dressed in cream suits.

"This is music!" said Njekwa, nodding her head.

"This is just noise," Charles complained.

"This is pure African music. Look, even the white people like it," she pointed at the sharp-nosed gentlemen who had his hands in his pocket.

"He's probably the manager of the group!"

She took his hands and took him closer to the stage to dance with him. Her dress swayed, brushing his trousers. He bent down to her ear.

"I love you," he said, a little harsher than he had intended.

All she did was give him a cheeky look. He loosened up a bit, but his dancing did not impress Njekwa.

That night, Charles was breathing against her neck warmly.

"Why don't you use your real name? Chialuka," Njekwa asked.

"I just don't." He kissed her back.

"It's a beautiful name. God has done a great work."

"It's the best way I can forget."

***

Mr Phiri's hands were failing him, his eyes were growing tired.

"I'm going to die before any of you give me a grandchild!" complained Mr Phiri to his two daughters. Frances had come over for a visit.

"I'm not yet ready to have children. Njekwa on the other hand is all set. You should be expecting bride price from Sanyambe by the end of the year."

Njekwa had not thought about Sanyambe since she began spending time with Charles. Her routine had been cleanly polished until it twinkled. She was happy with the way things were now. Njekwa invited Frances to her flat one evening.

"I proposed to cook an exotic meal for you but your sister refused," said Charles, pouring warm water over Frances' hands to wash them.

"I would have loved that, but I know how Njekwa gets in the kitchen, she really takes over."

"Not when it's my turn to cook. She watches TV while I prepare something to spoil her with."

Frances looked at Charles attentively, entranced by the gentleman that he was.

"When do you plan on marrying my sister? I hope it's soon, *Baba* wants grandchildren."

"*Iwe*!" said Njekwa as she tapped her sister's shoulder.

"What? It's the truth!"

When they had finished eating, they sat in the living room going through newspapers.

"I feel we are going to be independent soon," said Frances, closing her newspaper.

"And that's a good thing?" said Charles.

"Of course it is! Then we can finally have power over ourselves."

"That's what they did in Nigeria, now look where they are."

From then on, Njekwa steered the conversations, trying her best to shield Charles from Frances' spears.

Njekwa drove her sister home that night.

"If I were you, I'd sink my fingers into him and never let him go."

"Frances! We're still getting to know each other."

"Some people get married on the day they meet. I can see why you don't want us talking about Sanyambe. That man of yours is silver wrapped in gold."

Nancy came back from India two months after she left. They had buried her brother before she arrived in India; she spent the rest of her time there staying at her mother's new house. Njekwa looked for traces of sadness in her voice so she could comfort her friend but found none. Nancy was changed by her trip to India. She brought Njekwa a sari.

"Where am I going to wear this?"

"I'll throw us a party just so you can wear it."

Nancy was delighted to hear that Njekwa and Charles were spending time together. He had fit in perfectly, bloomed like sunflowers on the most unexpected of days.

One evening, Njekwa was in Nancy's kitchen.

"So when is the wedding?" Nancy joked, "I want to be the maid of honour!"

"You'll have to discuss that with my sister."

"I hope you're happy Jay."

"I am," she said, "He loves me."

***

One evening, while Njekwa and Charles drove back from a public lecture, he placed a hand on her leg.

"You need both hands to drive," she said.

He gave her leg a squeeze before placing it back on the steering wheel.

"I've been offered a fellowship in Minnesota." He paused briefly, "And I want you to come with me."

"What?"

"I leave in two weeks for the US to get acquainted, then after that, I come back. I want you to come with me. If it's a job you'd like, I can get one for you there, that's if you want one. If you want to go back to school, I can even arrange a place for you there. I just want to make sure you're going to be with me."

"This is too sudden."

"I knew you would feel that way. That's why I didn't ask you to marry me now even though I had planned to. But whenever you are ready for that, just let me know. You already know I love you."

Silence enfolded them.

"I'll think about it," she assured him.

Njekwa was there to see Charles off at the airport. She rushed back to her flat, gathering her scattered thoughts and emotions. Charles called her in two days to tell her about his trip. He hated flying but he claimed that his trip had been comfortable. He loved the city that he was in and he had already found a place to stay. He was happy with how accommodating the university was.

"It will be a good home for us," he told Njekwa.

"It's only been three days! You sound as if you've arrived in the Promised Land."

"It might be too early to say but I'm keeping an open mind. I'll bring you back something special."

The next day the phone rang, Njekwa thought Charles had caught the flu.

"I told you to take lots of warm clothing with you! Now look, you've caught the cold."

"Have you forgotten my voice that quickly?"

"Sanyambe?" In a few minutes her senses were lost.

"Haven't you heard that I was coming back?"

"I did." She thought for a second. "How did you get my number?"

"A man has his ways."

"Indeed, he does. So how have you been?"

"We can talk about that in person."

After a few minutes, Njekwa replaced the receiver and eased into the soft couch. She tried to recollect what had just occurred.

Njekwa arrived at the hotel just as the sun began to set. Sanyambe looked exotic sitting at the table, his arms crossed over the mosaic table, a plate of crisps and wine before him. He could easily be photographed for a travel guide. Njekwa thought she should leave before she even approached him. Sanyambe spotted Njekwa and approached her.

"Our food should be arriving soon, I ordered on your behalf."

"How did you know what I want?"

"I know you Njekwa," he said, taking her into his arms. His embrace was warm. They sat at the table and picked up from where they had left. He spoke about his experience at university in the UK and how he was homesick each day. She asked him why he didn't return home earlier. He explained how he felt it would be an embarrassment for him to return home after all of the investment he had put into going to school there. He would have felt like a defeated soldier. He made the choice to return to Southern Rhodesia only after he completed his degree.

"The first doctor from your family. Very impressive," said Njekwa.

"You'll never be fully appreciated out there."

She questioned in her mind if one of the reasons why he returned was for her.

"You haven't really changed Njekwa, you're still the same gentle soul that you were when I left."

She had changed a great deal. If he was not able to see that he was not very attentive. The rest of the evening passed by like a summer breeze, with fine music and delicious food. They took the same taxi back home. It arrived at Njekwa's flat first.

"So I'll see you around then?" said Sanyambe.

"Yes, I'll see you around." She stepped out of the taxi and immediately ran to her flat. She heard a knock on the door a few minutes later.

"What are doing here?" she asked Sanyambe who was framed perfectly by the door.

"I can't let any minute go to waste."

"Go home; you don't know what you are saying."

"I know exactly what I'm saying!"

He walked inside, Njekwa not trying to stop him. His kiss was full. His touch was sincere. His desire was true. They lay down on the floor, forgetting anything else that mattered or existed in the universe. For a few minutes after they were spent, they sat with their heads against the couch. Sanyambe lifted Njekwa up and placed her on the bed gently just like how flowers are laid on water. They laid next to each other and escaped into what felt like a trance.

Njekwa made sure to sneak Sanyambe out before the sun came up.

"Come to my hotel later," he said.

"You didn't have to ask at all!"

He sped off in a white taxi.

The afternoon sun found Njekwa in Sanyambe's hotel room. The Sanyambe that belonged to her in street alleys or stolen moments was now gone. The person in front of her was a man. They enjoyed the hotel's delicious offering of glazed potatoes and carefully roasted beef. He was a light eater which surprised Njekwa because of his full figure. He was happy to speak about anything that fascinated her which was a little of everything. They spoke about her workplace, and how she wanted to find a new place, to how softer his skin had become over the years.

In the evening, Sanyambe arrived at her doorstep with a suitcase.

"What do you need that for?"

"Last time I left without brushing my teeth or fresh clothes. Do you want a repeat of that?"

He wheeled the suitcase into the master bedroom. That night, she prepared a meal for him. Underneath her breath she uttered a prayer that neither Nancy nor anybody she knew would arrive on her doorstep. She dished out a stew of spicy fish.

"Are you a chef now?"

"You like my food?"

"You haven't answered my question," he said between chewing.

"Neither have you!"

That night they slept entangled to each other, each one as desperate for the other.

Things Fall Apart by Chinua Achebe was sitting on the table as they ate scrambled eggs in the morning.

"You're going to have to lend me this book, you know?" said Sanyambe.

"I'm not sure you'll enjoy it. It talks mainly about colonialism in West Africa."

"Then it's a very important read. I've been looking for it everywhere and I can never find it." She slid the book towards him and studied the cover, "The author is Ghanaian, is he not?"

"Nigerian," said Sanyambe. Njekwa appeared as if she had seen a phantom. "What's the matter with you?"

"Nothing," she responded.

The phone rang a few minutes later, then she picked up the phone hastily.

"My love," uttered Charles.

"Charles, what time is it there?"

"It's four in the morning."

"You should be asleep," her tone was almost frustrated.

"And you should be right here with me! The university is great here and I'm sure you'll like the surrounding city."

"That's good for you."

"I'll be back soon and we can talk more clearly about this, okay? I love you." There was a pause. "Whenever you're ready."

Sanyambe shouted across the flat. Njekwa did not make an effort to block the receiver. He kept shouting until Njekwa told Charles that she had to go.

"We'll speak later," she said.

***

That night as they sat in front of the television, Njekwa had her head on Sanyambe's lap.

"My father is dying for grandchildren before he passes. My brother isn't ready to settle down and Francis is waiting for some mythical Prince Charming to fall from the heavens. I suppose I'll be the first to give him a grandchild. Imagine that? The last born is the first to make them grandparents."

"I've always thought you'd be a good mother," said Sanyambe.

"I wouldn't know how many children you would want, one is just fine with me!"

Sanyambe did not respond. Njekwa turned her head to look at her companion. Her head was already on a tailspin before he said what he had to say.

"My family is arranging for me to have a Lozi bride."

"What?"

"Did you not hear what I said? I should be getting married sooner rather than later."

"Why are you here then?"

"I wanted to spend time with you before I was married. And I had missed you very, very much, believe me."

"I believe you! But why not me? Am I not Lozi enough for you? Just because my mother is a native of this country?"

Njekwa stood up.

"You're not the proper kind that we are looking for." He made it appear as if she was a pair of shoes on display.

"You're just like me, we both grew up here in this country and we have the same ideals."

"It's about blood, Njekwa and look at you! You're too…modern. My parents would want somebody more traditional."

She stormed off and slept over at Charles' flat that night. For the first time ever, she could not recall her dream. The next morning when she returned to her flat Sanyambe was gone and so had his belongings. He had left *Things Fall Apart*.

***

Nancy placed a lot of distance between them as Njekwa recounted the past few days.

"What were you thinking?" asked Nancy.

"I wasn't."

"That's obvious!"

"Well, it's over now."

"So you're just going to move on as if nothing happened?"

"Yes, what else can I do?" she pleaded.

"You cheated on Charles!"

As if she needed somebody to say it out loud. As if the magnitude of her actions did not weigh her down sorely. As if she did not have to face Charles later that day to talk about the issue. When the time finally came, Charles' door was unlocked and she entered to find him sitting on the couch, reading the newspaper. She sat across from him.

"How was your trip?" she asked.

"Who is he?"

"A friend of mine from when I was younger." He remained quiet. "We were together for only three days."

"So you forgot about us for three days?"

"I never forgot you. Besides, it was a stupid mistake."

"You must take me for a fool when I say I love you, don't you? And that you're all I have."

After that, Njekwa returned to her flat feeling pain all around her. All she could do was cry. Charles began to wake up very early in the morning so that we wouldn't have to see her. At night, he came home late, some nights close to midnight. After two weeks, Njekwa found Charles' front door ajar. She arrived to find his flat empty, the walls bare and the floor clean.

Two months floated by like feathers in the air. Since she had told Nancy about the three days with Sanyambe, the two of them hardly spoke. Her mother had told her that Sanyambe had left a wedding invitation for their family.

"Will you be attending?" Nancy mocked.

"Will you go with me? Maybe we can convince the bride to make you a bridesmaid."

They both laughed.

"What are you going to do? Really?" Nancy asked.

Njekwa dialled a number that afternoon.

"Hello?" said the voice on the other end.

"Charles…"

"Yes, how can I help you?"

"I'm ready."

SOMETHING ONLY I KNOW

I know why Nakai died. Of course, I am not going to tell anybody. Being the only one who knows makes me feel indomitable.

Her body was discovered on the hotel curb. They ruled that it was a suicide. *'Prostitute throws herself outside of window'* the headlines read. I had to find out about my best friend's death in the newspapers. To this day I do not know whether anybody cared to bury her. Of course, me and the rest of the girls mourned her death, but not for too long.

Nakai was not a person you would think sold her body to men. She was ethereal in every respect of the word. She had the kind of skin you imagined only wet clay could look and feel like; it seemed as if each day water journeyed across her skin, smoothing it out evenly. Her eyes were clear sheets of glass. Her back arched like the crescent moon while her head was held high like a royal's. Even Mama had a certain subtle respect for Nakai which extended to me due to my association with Nakai.

We got along well with the rest of the girls we lived with and we spoke to each other freely. We would joke about which cars were the most comfortable to do the deed. On that matter, we unanimously agreed that older model cars with seat finishes made of cloth were the most comfortable.

"Those Mercedes Benzes with leather seats are so uncomfortable!"

"I need to send money back to my mother and son."

"The government has not given us jobs so we are forced to do this job."

"He only wanted to sleep with me if he heard me speaking Ndebele! Imagine *kupenga kwakadii ikoko?*"

"My mother died when I was young. This was the quickest way for me to get out of the house." This was me. That was when my bond with Nakai was formed. She had also lost her mother at a young age. I did not know any other details about her personal life except this fact.

After four years of prostitution she, and I were now considered old women and the younger girls were trickling onto the streets, some as young as twelve years old, were now stealing our customers. One night a thirteen-year-old girl got into a fight with another prostitute in her mid-thirties. If I had not intervened, I don't know how it would have ended.

"*Vari kutibira ma*customers *edu vana ava*," the woman had complained. I had wanted to tell the girl to stop what she was doing but I had no right to give any kind of moral advice. That was when I started speaking to Nakai about finding something better to do.

We would not be the first to leave the trade. There was Netsai who came back one day, traumatised because she claimed she had been picked up by a Satanist who had a snake suck at her breast. She showed us the snake bites herself. Then there was Stella who met a man who was willing to sponsor her so she could finish her O Levels. Of course I will never forget Susan who left the day after her best friend was murdered by her regular customer who allegedly thought she had stolen from him. Her body was dumped on our front gate.

We spoke the day I had gone to the clinic with her to get a pregnancy test. I suggested opening a boutique in the city centre where we would sell only the most beautiful clothes on the market. She suggested we could start a stall where we would sell vegetables. As we juggled around more ideas, she told me the reason why Nakai died; she was in love with a client.

"It's perfect my friend! Now I have my best friend and the man of my dreams and a future full of opportunities. He can sponsor whatever dream we have."

He was different, she told me. He was a regular of hers and she could tell that he felt something for her. It sounded more like *she* felt something special for him.

And now she is dead. Nakai had plans and dreams and we were going to turn our lives around. She could not have killed herself and left me alone like this, I know it. I vowed to myself that I was going to find him.

One day, I was the only girl on the street and Nakai's regular, the 'love of her life' arrived. I hopped into his truck and we went to a nearby lodge. He was easy to look at. He was gentle in his actions, from the way he closed the door, the way he led me slowly to the bed, the way he asked me if I wanted something to eat.

"Or would you prefer something to drink?"

I told him I wasn't thirsty. He brought my face in alignment with his and laid me slowly on the bed. I felt my hands form into fists prepared to harm him.

"I lost someone important, I just need to forget."

I asked what had happened.

"She died a horrible death." He cupped his face into his hands and turned away from me.

"Please excuse me," I zoomed into the bathroom and locked the door.

Looking into the bathroom mirror an hour later, I was in doubt. I was going to take the life of this man with strong conviction that he was the reason for Nakai's death. He called me from the bathroom asking me if everything was alright. He was lying on the bed, his necktie removed.

"Why did she die?" I asked.

"She knew too much," he said, "Just like you're about to learn too much."

ARRIVALS

Chohuma could not believe her ears when she heard that the two men had been shot by the white man's guns. She could not imagine anything powerful enough to penetrate her brother's iron chest. The bodies were brought back a week after the revolt.

The village could not decide whether to be sad, ashamed or both. The men had brought nothing back to justify their stubbornness except blood-stained bodies. Chohuma's sister, Shingaidzo, was now left with two sons who did not have a father. The world that she knew had turned upside down. Where were the ancestral spirits that were supposed to guard the men as they entered the mouth of the lion? She stopped believing in them as the days went on and secretly found a new god, the god of the white man. Chohuma attended the meetings held by the white men who called themselves missionaries in secret, afraid of what her family would do to her if they found out.

Chohuma had seen a number of villagers gather around the missionaries like ants gathering on a drop of honey. They were taught how to speak English and of the one living God. Curiosity had bitten her mind and the wound did not let her heal until she attended her first meeting at a place they called a church, built by large poles and black plastic. She was particularly enchanted by Gideon, the only black missionary that was part of the team. His dark skin had the smoothness of air, his hair was black as the ash-stained pots and he stood tall like the village kings. What struck her most was the way he spoke in English, each sentence cascading easily into the next without much thought. It was Gideon who made Chohuma eager to speak this odd language that had crossed over from beyond the mountains. She memorised verses quickly from the book they had brought with them.

To make sure nobody told her family about her visits to the mission, she did not speak to the other villagers who came so that they would not know her name. The only person who knew that she came was Shingaidzo. She would not allow herself to get married in the fashion her other sisters had been married. She had to break free from people who were leading her to the place she had come to know as hell.

She believed she could no longer keep this new discovery a secret any longer, so she decided to tell her family. After she had told her parents about her new practice, Chohuma's father slapped her across the face. He cursed her for disgracing their culture and nearly beat her into silence. Chohuma made her way to Gideon and told him of what had happened. He took her into his arms and held her tightly as her tears settled on his white shirt. She was reassured of their teachings, "Blessed are you, when men shall revile you, and persecute you, and shall say all manner of evil against you falsely, for my sake". He reassured her of the wisdom she had above her elders. Gideon allowed Chohuma to live and work at the mission. She agreed, vowing to return to her family one day to show them the light.

Chohuma was given some of the beautiful garments to cover herself. Wearing them made her feel holier and closer to the God who had brought about civilisation. She memorised each prayer by heart, eagerly waiting for the day that she would be brought into her new life. When she would become a new creature. That time finally came when she was baptised.

"I baptise you in the name of the father and of the son and of the holy-spirit," said the priest, Father Alexander, as he poured water over Chohuma's forehead. She expected to feel a flush of newness sweep across her body. Instead she felt coldness upon her brow. From that day onwards they would call her Ruth. To Gideon, it seemed that her new name had always been there. He spoke it without having to think twice about it, like she did for the weeks that followed her baptism. This was her new life, the life she had chosen, not a life dictated by her birth. Ruth worked dutifully for the missionaries, cleaning their small camp, washing their clothes and preparing their meals. She had been taught how to do most of these duties by another woman called Anna who had joined the church.

Gideon was often away on missions he called evangelism. She once asked him whether she could join him on the expeditions. She thought that if she learned how to evangelise like Gideon, she could do it with her family. He told her she was not yet ready to carry tasks like that. Gideon made another proposal to her; he asked her to be his wife. She was surprised to hear that a man such as him would want to be married to her. Ruth agreed with little to no apprehension. Father Alexander was more than delighted to wed the two in the small church building which was still under construction. Only a handful of people attended the ceremony, yet happiness filled the room. After the ceremony, Gideon continued with his evangelism work while she stayed in the missionary to refine herself.

The joy of Ruth's pregnancy was only increased by the arrival of Shingaidzo to the missionary. Shingaidzo had left her new husband and started taking her baptism classes, eager to be born again like her sister. She told Ruth that their father resisted any news that came from the white men. It was by the grace of God they managed to meet up, according to Ruth. Ruth would teach Shingaidzo everything that was necessary for her to be a perfect fit for this new place. Shangaidzo was also very helpful to her sister, advising and monitoring her pregnancy with rigour.

The time finally arrived when Ruth gave birth to a son. The nurse gave Ruth a sorry look as she handed her the infant. When she looked down at her child, he was not breathing or even crying. She ran her fingers across the child's soft lips and tiny nose trying to get a response but failed. Not only had she failed to resurrect the child with her desire for him to live, but she also failed Gideon by giving him a child that was dead. Gideon only looked at the child once before leaving the room.

The day the church building was complete was the day her child was buried. Only Father Alexander, Gideon, Ruth, Anna and Shingaidzo were there to bury him. The priest poured holy water over the shallow grave that had been dug up at the back of the church. Ruth wanted to give herself a few minutes more at the grave, to bring herself to believe that this was truly the will of God. She would go to confession after this, she had not prayed in the last two nights and had to bring herself back to salvation.

She entered the confessional and knelt. "Bless me father for I have sinned; my last confession was six days ago… I cursed the name of God."

***

Gideon left without telling Ruth where he was going. She still had not asked for his forgiveness. She thought of how

David had lost his first son with Bathsheba but they had their next child who became the king of Israel. Gideon finally returned after three days of absence. They did not say much to each other the night he returned. Gideon did not finish the food that was prepared for supper. Ruth finally asked for Gideon's forgiveness.

"Did you ask for God's forgiveness?" Gideon asked

"Yes, I did."

"Good. Only his forgiveness matters."

She followed him to the bedroom where he had already undressed and put out the light. Ruth undressed quickly and moved into the bed next to him.

When Shingaidzo appeared at Ruth's door the next afternoon, Ruth could not believe how badly beaten she was. She was even more surprised when Shingaidzo informed her that Gideon was the one who had beaten her. Her face was swollen with lumps that looked as if they were about to burst any second. Her eyes were bloodshot and she had scratch marks on her arms.

"You must be confused. Gideon could not have done this to you."

"I know what I saw." Shingaidzo paused as Ruth wiped the blood off of her neck, "It was him. He came onto me like a demon."

"Do not speak of my husband like that."

Shingaidzo wanted to leave at that moment. Her own sister had not listened to her story but chose to support the man that nearly killed her.

"He is my husband. We are one flesh and I will always be there to defend him until I die."

"Remember what our elders say, *rina manyanga hariputirwe*. You may not choose to believe me, but the truth will come to light soon enough."

"What elders? The only elder that you are accountable to is God. Don't forget that. To think I did my best to help you escape that life of darkness."

Shingaidzo left the house in a rush.

Gideon came back home after Ruth had finished praying. She dished out supper for the two of them and cleaned up the kitchen. Ruth was hesitant to ask him about her sister. She was unsure of how to do it without offending him. Ruth mentioned that Shingaidzo had passed by earlier on during the day, her body battered.

"Did she tell you it was me who did it?"

"Gideon what are you saying?" She did not want to believe him.

"She is the reason why we lost the baby."

"Where did you hear that from?"

"I went to visit a *n'anga* those days I was gone. He told me that it was the arrival of your sister that caused you to lose the child. She came with some medicines from your village and cast them on you."

This was the man who had spoken such fluent English, surrendered himself to God completely who was telling her this. Ruth did not question him on his actions because it was clear from his voice he was not lying.

"But we are taught to have no other God besides Him and you decided to go to a witchdoctor! I am very disappointed in you, Gideon. You spend your time away from me preaching the gospel but you then seek out other gods!"

Gideon stood up, his eyes black and his fists filled with iron. He grabbed Ruth's arms and brought her towards him.

His wide pores and curly moustache became so defined in Ruth's eyes.

"Who is it that taught you of this God? Was it not me? If it wasn't for me you would have been married off to another pagan village rat. My generosity is what brought you here; you don't get to question me on my actions unless you want to dig your own grave."

Ruth opened her mouth to speak, but Gideon slapped the words out of her mouth. He left her on the floor as she wept without a sound. The tears were dried up as she left for the bedroom where her husband had already slipped into bed. In the creeping light on the moon, Ruth undressed and lay on the bed, searching out her mind. Searching for true light.

Acknowledgements

'Family Affairs' was previously published in *Mosi oa Tunya Literary Review*
'The woman with the twisted hair' was previously published in *House of Mutapa* and the *African Writer Review*
'Strange Things' was published in *Unspoken Articles*.

First and foremost, I must thank God for the inspiration to write these stories and the courage to get them published. Thank you to Carnelian Heart Publishing for giving me this glorious moment in the sun, particularly to Samantha Rumbidzai Vazhure for her reassurance and guidance and Panashe Lazarus Nyagwambo for refining the book to become what it is now.

I want to thank every friend, family member and acquaintance I have. Each of you have influenced me and ultimately this body of work in one way or another. I realise the importance of gratitude because it shows that nobody ever makes it alone.

It takes a lot to put any piece of art together (years even!) and one of the lessons I have learned sitting down with these characters is the commonality of our human experience. These are stories of people who are unloved, unwanted and unheard; many emotions I confront daily. This book is a reassurance that nobody is ever alone and that our experience here on earth might be more similar than we thought!

Happy reading.

About the author

Kudzai Mhangwa lives and writes from his home in Harare, Zimbabwe. He writes poetry, plays, short stories and essays. He is the winner of the 2021 Intwasa Short Story Prize. *Moments in the Private Room* is his first collection of short stories.

9 781914 287428